TOAD RAGE

Morris Gleitzman

Galaxy

CHIVERS PRESS
BATH

First published 1999
by
Penguin Books Australia Ltd
This Large Print edition published by
Chivers Press
by arrangement with
Penguin Books Ltd
2003

ISBN 0 7540 7844 2

British Library Cataloguing in Publication Data

Gleitzman, Morris

Toad rage.—Large print ed.
1. Children's stories 2. Large type books
I. Title
823.9'14[J]

ISBN 0-7540-7844-2

Printed and bound in Great Britain by
BOOKCRAFT, Midsomer Norton, Somerset

For Mary-Anne

'Uncle Bart,' said Limpy. 'Why do humans hate us?'

Uncle Bart looked down at Limpy and smiled fondly.

'Stack me, Limpy,' he chuckled, 'you are an idiot.'

Limpy felt his warts prickle with indignation as Uncle Bart hopped onto the road after a bull ant.

No wonder I've never heard any other cane toad ask that question, thought Limpy, if that's the reply you get.

Limpy was glad the grass at the edge of the highway was taller than he was. At least the millions of insects flying around the railway crossing light couldn't see who Uncle Bart was calling an idiot.

'Humans don't hate us,' Uncle Bart

was saying, his mouth full of bull ant and grasshopper. 'What are you on about? Stack me, some of the dopey ideas you youngsters come up with . . .'

Limpy waited patiently for Uncle Bart to finish. Uncle Bart was his fattest uncle, and his bossiest. When Uncle Bart had a point to make, he liked to keep on making it until you gave in and looked convinced.

Tonight, though, Limpy didn't give in.

He didn't have to. While Uncle Bart was getting his mucus in a knot about how humans definitely didn't hate cane toads, a truck came roaring round the corner in a blaze of lights, straightened up, rumbled through the railway crossing, swerved across the road straight at Uncle Bart and drove over him.

Limpy trembled in the grass while the truck thundered past in a cloud of diesel fumes and flying grit. Then he hopped onto the road and looked down at what was left of Uncle Bart.

The light overhead was very bright because it had a whole railway crossing to illuminate, and Limpy was able to see very clearly that Uncle Bart wasn't his fattest uncle any more.

Flattest more like, he thought sadly.

'See,' he said quietly to Uncle Bart. 'That's what I'm on about.'

'Har har har,' chortled a nearby grasshopper. 'Your uncle's a placemat. Serves him right.'

Limpy ignored the grasshopper and turned to watch the truck speeding away into the darkness. From the movement of its tail lights he could tell it was weaving from side to side. Each time it weaved, he heard the distant 'pop' of another relative being run over.

'Yay,' shouted the grasshopper. 'More placemats.'

Limpy sighed.

He decided not to eat the grasshopper. Mum was always warning him he'd get a belly ache if he ate when he was upset or angry.

To take his mind off Uncle Bart, Limpy crossed the road to have a look at Uncle Roly.

Uncle Roly was extremely flat too,

but at least he was smiling.

Which is what you'd expect, thought Limpy sadly, from your kindest uncle, even when he has been dead for two nights.

Limpy reached forward and gently prodded Uncle Roly. He was dry and stiff. The hot Queensland sun had done its job.

Limpy remembered how Uncle Roly had never been dry and stiff when he was alive. He'd always had a warm smile for everyone, even the family of holiday-makers two evenings ago who'd purposely aimed their car straight for him down the wrong side of the road.

'Oh, Uncle Roly,' whispered Limpy. 'Couldn't you see the way they were looking at you?'

Limpy shuddered as he remembered the scary expressions on the holiday-makers' faces. It was exactly the same look of hatred that had been on the face of the truck driver who'd tried to kill Limpy when he was little.

I was lucky, thought Limpy sadly. When it happened to me I'd only just finished being a tadpole. I had a pair of brand-new legs and I could hop almost completely out of the way. I only got one leg a bit squashed. Poor old Uncle Roly was completely flat before he knew what hit him.

Limpy felt his crook leg start to ache, as it often did when he was sad and stressed. He gazed down at Uncle Roly's very wide smile and felt his throat sac start to wobble.

Why?

Why would a car-load of humans purposely kill an uncle who had such a good heart that he was still smiling two nights after being run over by a station wagon and caravan?

I don't get it, thought Limpy. I can understand why grasshoppers and other insects don't like us. It's because we eat them. But we don't eat humans. We can't even fit them into our mouths. So why do they hate us?

Limpy felt his warts tingle with determination.

One day, he thought, I'll go to a human place and find out why and try to do something about it, even if I end up dry and stiff and flat myself.

The thought made him feel weak and sick.

'Time to go home, Uncle Roly,' he said.

Limpy picked Uncle Roly up, heaved him onto his shoulders, and hopped slowly back across the road to Uncle Bart.

'Bye, Uncle Bart,' said Limpy to the damp layer of pressed skin and flat warts on the tarmac. 'I'll be back for you when you've dried out.'

He wondered if he'd find the courage to visit the humans before he saw Uncle Bart again.

I need to get braver, he thought. But how?

'Rack off, placemat,' yelled the grasshopper.

Ignoring all thoughts of belly ache, Limpy ate him.

Practice, thought Limpy as he chewed, that's how.

‘Oh no, Limpy,’ said Mum in exasperation. ‘You haven’t brought home another dead relative.’

Limpy was too puffed to answer. Although the swamp where he lived wasn’t very far from the highway, it was still a long haul for a skinny toad with a crook leg and a dried uncle on his back.

‘Well, just don’t leave him lying around in your room,’ said Mum. ‘That room’s a pigsty. I’m sick of tidying up dead relatives in there.’

‘Mum,’ said Limpy. ‘Uncle Roly’s your brother. Don’t you care that he’s been run over?’

Mum gave a big sigh and leaned against the leaf she’d been preparing dinner on. She put down the ants she’d been stuffing slugs with and closed her eyes.

When she opened them, Limpy could see her throat sac was trembling.

'Oh, Limpy,' she said quietly. 'Of course I care. But I've got hundreds of brothers and sisters. If I let myself get upset every time one of them's run over, I'll be a nervous wreck.'

Limpy felt a hand grip his shoulder.

He jumped.

For a second he thought Uncle Roly had come back to life and was desperate for a drink of water.

Then he realised it was Dad.

'Mum's right, son,' said Dad. 'You've got to accept the facts of life. Highway lights attract flying insects, so that's where we've got to go for a feed.'

'But there's heaps of other food here in the swamp,' said Limpy. 'There's worms in the mud and slugs in the water and spiders in the mangroves and termites in the paperbarks and dung beetles in the . . .'

'Limpy,' interrupted Mum, 'you know perfectly well you need flying insects for a balanced diet. How many times have we told you that you won't grow up big and strong unless you eat your flying insects?'

Limpy sighed. She was right.

'And in these parts,' said Dad, 'the highway is where the flying insects are. It's just bad luck that humans use highways too. All we can do is accept it. It's the way it's been since the dawn of time.'

'But why do they hate us, Dad?' said Limpy. 'Why do they go out of their way to run us over?'

Dad thought hard for a long time. Then he gave an exasperated shrug.

'It's just the way things are,' he said to Limpy. 'Now go and tidy your room and don't worry your dopey old head about it.'

* * *

I can't help worrying about it, thought Limpy miserably as he pushed his way through the big tropical leaves into his room. It's just the way I am.

He carefully lifted Uncle Roly onto the uncle stack.

I don't know what Mum's moaning

about, Limpy said to himself. I don't reckon my room's that untidy.

He looked around at the neat piles of rellies. Uncles by the bed. Aunts in the corner. Cousins next to the mud patch.

The only way I could make these tidier, he thought, is if I had some of those racks.

He'd seen a picture of the racks in a newspaper that had been chucked out of a passing car. Humans used them for storing round flat metal things, but Limpy could see they'd be perfect for dead rellies.

He straightened up Uncle Roly on the uncle stack. In a couple of days he'd be adding Uncle Bart to it.

Poor old Uncle Bart, thought Limpy. He spent most of his life saying 'stack me' and soon I will be.

A voice interrupted his sad thoughts.

'Limpy.'

Limpy turned round.

Mum and Dad had followed him in to his room.

He started to tell them about the racks, but they didn't give him a chance.

'Limpy,' said Mum, gently. 'I know we get a bit cross with you sometimes, but we just want to say that we're really glad you're still around.'

They both gave him a hug.

Limpy glowed with pleasure. Most of his brothers and sisters had been swept away from home ages ago, when they were still blobs of spawn, and sometimes he worried he was a bit of a burden to Mum and Dad.

'If you ever got flattened, you know, more than you have been already,' said Dad, 'we'd be really, really sad.'

Limpy glowed even more.

He started to tell them he felt the same about them, but just the thought of a Mum and Dad stack made his throat ache so much he had to stop.

Instead he said, 'And Charm too?'

Mum smiled. 'Of course,' she said. 'We're glad she's still around too.'

Limpy glowed again. A lot of parents were ashamed of kids like Charm. Kids who'd stayed small because of pollution. But he could tell by looking at Mum and Dad's faces that they loved his younger sister as much as they did him.

'Where is Charm?' he said. 'I haven't seen her since I got back.'

'She went down to the highway,' said Mum, 'to get me some mozzies for dessert.'

Limpy stared at her in panic.

'She shouldn't be going to the highway,' he said. 'She's too young.'

'She's got to learn to collect food like everyone else,' said Dad. 'Anyway, she'll be fine. She's with Goliath.'

Limpy felt anxiety stab through his glands.

Not cousin Goliath.

Anyone but cousin Goliath.

Limpy tried to make a frantic dash through the leaves and off in the direction of the highway, forgetting that if he hopped too fast his crook leg made him go in circles.

He grimaced with frustration. This is the one drawback, he thought as he staggered around the room, of having one leg shorter than the other.

He crashed into a stack of rellies. Uncles rolled in all directions.

'Calm down,' said Dad. 'Charm'll be OK. Goliath'll look after her. He's big and strong and sensible.'

'Big, yes,' Limpy wanted to shout. 'Strong, yes. But can someone who sits in the middle of the road and tries to wee on passing traffic really be described as sensible?'

Limpy didn't have time to stand around shouting.

In the distance, from the direction of the highway, he heard the faint sound of a sixteen-wheeler slamming on its air brakes.

He had to get to Charm before it was too late.

Limpy's head was spinning by the time he got to the highway, partly because he was out of breath and partly because he'd been round in so many circles.

It didn't matter.

He could see Charm and she was OK.

So far.

She was sitting in the moonlight in the middle of the road, a small figure next to a much larger one.

Limpy peered anxiously at the hulking figure of Goliath at her side and saw he was holding a stick.

'Oh no,' groaned Limpy.

His warts prickled with fear.

He could feel the vibrations of an approaching vehicle.

If he didn't act quickly, Charm and

Goliath wouldn't be OK for much longer.

'Charm,' he yelled, but it just came out as a desperate croak. He hurled himself at her, but found himself going round in circles again.

Then Charm looked up, saw him, and hopped over, eyes bright with pleasure.

'G'night, Limpy,' she said, smiling up at him. 'How's it going?'

Limpy stared at her weakly.

'You could have been killed,' he said. 'What were you doing?'

'Goliath's got a plan,' she replied. 'He said he wants to show the humans that we're not going to take them running us over lying down.'

Limpy sighed. When they were handing out brains, Goliath must have swapped his for extra warts.

Limpy could feel the vehicle getting closer.

Goliath was facing the direction it was coming from, gripping his stick like a spear.

'Goliath,' yelled Limpy. 'Don't be a dope.'

Goliath ignored him.

Headlights swung round the bend in the highway and came towards them, bathing Goliath in dazzling white. Goliath rose unsteadily on his back legs.

'Mongrels,' he yelled, waving his stick at the oncoming lights. 'Big bums.'

Limpy started hopping towards Goliath.

Not too fast, he told himself. Stay in a straight line.

He got to Goliath with only a couple of wobbles, reached up, grabbed Goliath's big warty shoulders and tried to drag him off the road.

It was no good. Goliath was too much of a lump.

Then Limpy realised Charm was next to him and she was yanking at Goliath's leg.

'I was trying to tell him this was dopey when you arrived,' she panted.

Together they managed to drag the protesting Goliath across the bitumen.

'Hey,' yelled Goliath indignantly. 'You're spoiling my ambush.'

'Ambush?' puffed Limpy. 'You can't ambush a vehicle.'

'Yes I can,' retorted Goliath. 'I've planned it all out. At the last minute I'm gunna hop to one side and smash the windscreen and rip the doors off and demolish the engine.'

'Goliath,' wheezed Limpy as they all collapsed in the grass, 'you're a cane toad. That's a stick. A vehicle's about a thousand times bigger than you.'

Goliath, his warts glowing with determination, glared at Limpy.

'I can still give the duco a really nasty scratch.'

'Not,' said Limpy, 'if you're being flattened by a large number of radial tyres.'

'Limpy's right, Goliath,' said Charm. 'You should have thought about that.'

Goliath, frowning, thought about it now.

'I'll stab the tyres with the stick till they explode,' he said, 'and then those mongrels'll drive off the road and get smothered by their own air bags.'

The vehicle, a car, roared past. It swerved slightly and thumped over an aunt in the exact spot where Goliath had been sitting.

They all stared at the flat aunt.

Limpy gave a sad sigh.

There was a long silence.

'Yeah, well, she didn't have a stick, did she?' Goliath muttered finally.

His bulging shoulders sagged.

'Poor Aunty Violet,' said Charm.

Limpy looked at his little sister's sad face and felt his warts tingle with love and then prickle with worry.

It could have been Charm.

Limpy had an awful vision of her out on the tarmac night after night, proudly collecting her own food while huge trucks and convoys of holidaymakers swerved across the road and aimed straight at her.

Unless, thought Limpy, I can find a way to stop humans hating us.

Suddenly he knew he couldn't put it off any longer.

Not till next month, not till next week, not till he'd had time to get braver and make a will.

He had to start tonight.

Limpy found Ancient Eric at the far end of the swamp, eating a snake.

'Go away,' said Ancient Eric, 'I'm having my tea.'

Limpy had expected something like that. Ancient Eric, as well as being the oldest and wisest cane toad in the district, was also the grumpiest.

It must be hard to stay cheerful when you look like that, thought Limpy sympathetically.

Even though the moon was behind a cloud, Limpy could see just how unkind age had been to Ancient Eric. His poor old body was a disaster. The years had shrunk his skin and turned it tragically smooth. You could see his muscles rippling when he moved. He didn't have a wrinkle or a crease or a decent-sized wart on him.

Poor thing, thought Limpy.

Ancient Eric paused in the middle of getting the snake down his throat.

'You still here?' he said.

'I won't take up much of your time, Mr Eric,' said Limpy. 'I just want to ask your advice.'

Ancient Eric gulped the snake down a bit further.

'What advice?' he said.

'Well,' said Limpy, 'I was wondering if you knew where I could find some humans.'

For a moment Limpy thought Ancient Eric was going to choke.

'What do you want with humans?' demanded Ancient Eric when he'd recovered and swallowed the snake.

'I want to try and find out why they hate us so much,' said Limpy. 'So I can try and do something about it.'

Ancient Eric thought about this for a long while. Then he spoke.

'I'll tell you why humans hate us,' he said in a low voice.

Limpy moved closer.

'Humans hate us,' whispered Ancient Eric, 'because they've always hated us. It's the way things are. We have to accept it, just like we have to accept that flying insects are attracted to highway lights and crawling insects are attracted to wombat poo. It's a fact of life.'

Limpy sighed. He remembered that Dad had been one of Ancient Eric's students.

The snake stuck its head out of Ancient Eric's mouth and rolled its eyes.

'You're not listening to him, wart-brain,' it said to Ancient Eric. 'The young bloke doesn't want to accept that his loved ones are going to end up as waffles. He wants to go on a quest to discover great truths that will bring peace and security to cane toads for countless generations to come. Got it?'

The snake made scornful noises as if it couldn't believe it was being eaten by such an idiot.

'Do you mind?' snapped Ancient Eric to the snake. 'When I want advice from my dinner, I'll ask for it. Get back inside.'

The snake rolled its eyes again and

slithered back down Ancient Eric's throat.

'He's right,' said Limpy quietly. 'That is what I want to do.'

'See,' said a muffled voice from inside Ancient Eric.

Ancient Eric leaned forward and turned his head so one angry pink eye glared straight at Limpy.

'I know exactly what you want to do, young man,' rumbled Ancient Eric. 'I'm just trying to save your scrawny neck.'

Limpy opened his mouth to protest, but Ancient Eric didn't give him a chance.

'What do you think would happen if I told you where you could find humans?' he continued in a voice that sent shivers down Limpy's glands. 'If I told you about a place up the highway to the north where humans stop to put petrol in their cars? A place so far away, even I haven't been there. A place so dangerous, no cane toad has ever returned from it more than two centimetres thick. What do you think would happen if a young squirt like you tried to go there and make contact with humans, eh?'

Limpy shivered, even though the night air was as warm as mouse blood.

'Two words,' said Ancient Eric. 'Count them. First word, horrible. Second word, death.'

Limpy's throat sac was quivering so much he thought for a moment his dinner wanted to join in the conversation too.

'Understand?' demanded Ancient Eric.

Limpy nodded.

'Are you sure?'

Limpy nodded again.

'Then go away.'

Limpy couldn't move. He tried to open his skin pores as much as possible to get more oxygen into his body. Mum was always telling him to do that when he was rigid with anxiety.

After a bit his throat sac relaxed just enough for him to speak.

'There is just one more thing, Mr Eric,' he croaked.

'What?' grunted Ancient Eric.

Trembling, Limpy looked Ancient

Eric straight in the eye.

'Which way is north?'

'The petrol station?' gasped Charm.

She stared up at him, eyes wide with horror.

'You can't go there, it's too dangerous,' she pleaded. 'Goliath reckons there are humans there with fingernails the colour of blood, and some of them have got blue hair, and teeth that try and jump out of their mouths.'

'Shhh,' whispered Limpy. 'Keep your voice down. I don't want Mum and Dad to hear.'

He took Charm by the hand and led her out of her room and through the thick foliage to the edge of the swamp where they couldn't be overheard.

'Humans aren't like us,' said Charm desperately. 'They sleep at night and go out in the sun. Goliath reckons it's cause they've got small brains. What if they make you go out in the sun? You'll burn up.'

Limpy looked down at his sister's dear, anxious face.

'I'll stay in the shade,' he said gently. 'I'll get a pair of those black glasses humans wear. Don't worry.'

But he could see that Charm was very worried.

'What if it's too cold for you at night where humans live?' she said frantically. 'In our biology class Ancient Eric told us that humans make their own body heat. They plug themselves into electricity or something. Stuff we can't do. What if there's no warm rocks or bitumen for you to sit on. You'll catch a cold and die.'

'I'll find a sleeping human,' said Limpy, 'and sit on it.'

He tried not to let Charm see him shudder at the thought.

'You mustn't go,' pleaded Charm, flinging her arms round him. 'It's too dangerous.'

'I have to,' said Limpy. 'I have to try

and stop humans hating us.'

Gently he explained to her how none of the family would ever be safe until he did.

Charm frowned and nodded.

'OK then,' she said. 'I'm coming too.'

Limpy sighed. This was what he'd dreaded. Now he'd have to say stuff he'd rather not hear.

'You can't,' he said. 'Even though I'm going to be very careful not to get sunburnt or catch a cold, it still might be a little bit dangerous.'

He paused, wishing there was a less scary way of saying it.

There wasn't.

Limpy watched the faint light of dawn creep through the swamp. He found himself looking at his favourite climbing bush and his favourite mud-hole and his favourite patch of slimy moss, hazy in the soft grey light.

The memories that rippled through him were soft too, but they still made his glands ache.

Dad showing him how to eat a fresh-water prawn without getting the spikes up his nose.

Mum letting him and Charm make a slippery slide down her back.

Him and Charm making Mum and Dad wet themselves with laughter on family picnics by pretending to be mud worms with ticks in their tummies.

Limpy looked down at Charm's anxious face.

'It wouldn't be fair to Mum and Dad,' he whispered, 'if we both went and neither of us came back.'

Charm squeezed him even tighter. He put his arms round her and hugged her and felt like he never wanted to let her go.

'Don't worry,' he said, 'I will be coming back. That's what I want you to tell Mum and Dad. But wait till I'm far enough away that they can't try and stop me.'

Charm didn't say anything and for a moment he thought she was thinking of more reasons why he shouldn't go.

Please, he begged her silently, don't.

She didn't.

Instead she reached up and kissed him on the cheek.

'They'll be so proud when I tell

them,' she whispered. 'You think they don't care about what happens on the highway, but they do. I've seen Mum when she dusts your room. Sometimes she stops and puts her head in her hands.'

Limpy felt his eyes getting hot. He wanted to go to Mum right now and hold her head gently in his hands.

He didn't.

Charm kissed him on the other cheek.

'Bye,' she whispered. 'Be careful.'

'I will,' said Limpy, to himself as well as to her.

'You'll never make it,' sneered a blowfly, buzzing past Limpy's head. 'The petrol station's miles away. You'll get heat exhaustion and wander round in circles till you collapse in a heap and galahs peck your warts off.'

Limpy ignored the blowfly.

The day was too hot for snacks.

Instead he plodded on, wishing Queensland highways had big shady leaves next to them instead of straggly grass and sunbaked dirt that half-cooked your feet.

To take his mind off the scorching sun, Limpy tried to remember happy things. Like the top puddle he'd found in a shady ditch earlier on. He'd sat in it for ages, drinking in the delicious muddy water through his thirsty skin.

Now, plodding northwards, his

mouth felt dryer than a lizard's loungeroom.

'Give up, you big handbag,' yelled an ant. 'You haven't got a hope.'

Limpy changed his mind about snacks and his tongue shot out.

Ants were small, but they were juicy.

* * *

It was easier at night.

Limpy could smell water at night, and several times he found swamps not too far from the road.

Sitting in one, he closed his eyes for a rest and sadness bubbled up inside him like that gas you get from eating dung beetles.

He missed Charm. He'd never been away from her for a whole day and half a night before.

Limpy sighed.

He hoped she'd stay away from Goliath and traffic until he got back.

With a weary groan, Limpy dragged himself out of the swamp and headed north again.

As he trudged, to take his mind off

worrying about Charm, he worried about how hot the sun would be the next day.

*   *   *

The next day the sun was hot enough to melt a maggot.

Limpy staggered along the edge of the highway from one tiny patch of shade to the next, desperately wishing he had some of that white liquid humans rubbed on their skins in the sun.

He was so thirsty he'd drink anything.

Cars and trucks roared past, covering him with dust and fumes.

By the middle of the day he was almost a goner.

His head was spinning and he could see things shimmering on the road ahead. Stacks of flat rellies that vanished as you got closer. Pools of cool water that disappeared when you tried to walk through them. A red can with brown liquid dribbling out of it.

Limpy tried to walk through the can and banged his head.

It was real.

So was the liquid.

Limpy let it trickle over his skin and drank it in gratefully.

It left him very sticky, but able to trudge quite fast.

* * *

The sun was starting to get a bit lower, but nowhere near as low as Limpy's spirits.

As he plodded on he stared down at his legs. They were so tired they were numb.

He couldn't feel them.

It was like being a tadpole again.

Limpy wished he was a tadpole again, and that a bird would swoop down and snatch him up and fly to the petrol station with him in its beak.

Even in its lower digestive tract.

Anything so long as he didn't have to stagger any further.

Limpy wondered whether if he lay down and tucked his legs under him, birds would think he was a big tadpole.

He looked up to see if any big birds

were flying overhead.

Instead he saw, towering into the sky at last, the big plastic signs of the petrol station.

*   *   *

Limpy sat in the petrol station carpark, staring.

Not at the cars or the trucks or the buildings or the litter. At the area of bush fenced off next-door.

He'd never seen anything like it.

Inside the enclosure were kangaroos and koalas and emus and possums and parakeets and goannas and turtles and . . . and . . .

And humans.

Stack me, thought Limpy.

The humans were patting the kangaroos and stroking the koalas and grinning at the emus and winking at the possums and chatting with the parakeets and taking photos of the goannas and introducing their kids to the turtles.

At no stage was any human trying to run over any animal with any form of vehicle.

Limpy's heart was racing.

He started to hop towards the enclosure.

It was what he'd always dreamed of.

Friendly people.

He saw a group of humans standing next to a caravan at the edge of the carpark. He changed direction and hopped towards them.

No point competing with kangaroos, koalas and possums, he thought, when I can have this lot all to myself.

He wondered what they'd do first. Pat him? Stroke him? Introduce him to their kids?

One of the women in the group pointed to him and screamed.

Limpy stopped.

Perhaps she's just pleased and excited to see me, he thought hopefully.

But she didn't look very pleased.

She looked pretty upset.

So Limpy wasn't that surprised when the other humans in the group bent down, picked up rocks and charged at him.

Limpy hopped frantically in circles as rocks whizzed past him.

The humans were getting closer.

Limpy forced himself to slow down enough to hop straight. He flung himself into the thick undergrowth at the edge of the carpark.

Trembling, he crouched in the long grass while the people stamped around and shouted things.

He couldn't understand what they were saying, but he was pretty sure they weren't offering to share any ants with him.

After a while the people went back to their caravan.

Limpy stayed in the grass, weak with shock and disappointment.

I don't get it, he thought sadly. Humans can be friendly to possums and koalas, why can't they be friendly to cane toads?

A horrible thought hit him.

Perhaps, a long time ago, just after the dawn of time, a cane toad had done something really nasty to a human. Something so bad that humans had hated cane toads ever since and wanted to squash them at every opportunity.

If I knew what it was, thought Limpy, I could say sorry.

He struggled to think what it could have been.

Perhaps a human had chucked a can out of a car and a cane toad had chucked it back and hit the human on the head.

It didn't seem likely. Cane toads were pretty hopeless throwers.

Perhaps one of Goliath's ancestors had stabbed a car tyre with a stick and made the car drive off the highway and crash into a termites' nest.

That didn't seem likely either. If it had happened, humans would be going out of their way to drive over termites as well.

Perhaps humans were just jealous of

cane toads because cane toads had much longer tongues, which meant they got to eat all the juiciest insects and humans got left with the scaly centipedes and dust mites.

Limpy frowned.

It didn't seem enough, somehow.

Not for mass murder.

He knew there must be something else, something he hadn't thought of. He thought again till his head hurt, but it was no good, so he stopped worrying about the past.

Instead he worried about the future.

What I need, thought Limpy, is a way to make cane toads more popular with humans.

While he mulled this over, he watched a group of humans in the wildlife enclosure gazing at some big tropical butterflies. The humans had wide eyes and joyful smiles, and the butterflies looked pretty happy too.

Limpy sighed.

I wish I was a butterfly, he thought.

He looked down at his body and wondered if he could pretend to be a butterfly.

No hope. Even if he stretched the saggy skin under his armpits out as far as it would go, it still wouldn't look like wings in a million years.

Plus butterflies didn't have warts.

Limpy sighed again.

Suddenly the ground shook.

Limpy looked up fearfully. A huge truck was rumbling towards him. Limpy was about to turn and run when he saw that the truck was stopping.

He saw something else. Painted on the side of the truck was a large platypus and a large echidna and a large kookaburra.

Lucky things, thought Limpy. Some creatures are so popular with humans, they even get their own special trucks.

Then Limpy realised the platypus picture wasn't of a real platypus. It was a picture of a platypus costume with a human in it. Limpy could tell it was a human from the way the platypus was standing with its bottom sticking out.

Same for the echidna, and the kookaburra.

Limpy stared at the pictures, puzzled.

Why would humans want to disguise themselves as animals and birds?

He didn't get it, but he had to admit they were great disguises. The kookaburra's feathers and the echidna's spikes and the platypus's fur looked so real they'd even have fooled a kookaburra and an echidna and a platypus.

And, thought Limpy, a human behind a steering wheel.

Then Limpy had an idea that made his warts tingle with excitement.

An idea that made his long journey suddenly seem worth it.

An idea, he thought joyfully, that could keep Charm safe and bring peace and security to cane toads for countless generations to come.

* * *

The underpants were just what Limpy was looking for.

They had purple swirls on them and yellow blobs and green ripples and really bright orange around the edges.

Perfect, thought Limpy.

He had to have them.

The only problem was, they were lying on the floor of a parked caravan, just inside the open door.

Not just any caravan.

The rock-throwers' caravan.

Limpy hopped closer, warts prickling with fear, desperately hoping that the humans from the van were over in the enclosure, patting possums or chucking rocks at each other.

He hopped onto the caravan step and listened.

Nothing.

He hopped into the van and crept around a pair of furry slippers and sidled towards the underpants.

Suddenly a human voice boomed out.

Limpy went almost as flat as Uncle Roly, just from fear.

Then he saw something flickering in the gloom.

A human face in a box, speaking.

Other humans were lying in front of the box, asleep.

Limpy stared, relief flooding through his glands. He'd heard older family members talking about this box. Without it, they'd said gratefully, heaps more humans would be out at night driving over cane toads.

It was called telly.

Limpy was tempted to look at it for longer, but that would have been too dangerous, plus he had more important things to do.

He grabbed the underpants, leapt out the door and hopped under the van.

OK, he thought as he wriggled into the underpants, making sure that his body and head were completely covered, let's see if humans can be friendly to a cane toad if they think he's a tropical butterfly.

Limpy took a while to get into the wildlife enclosure, mostly because he couldn't see properly out of the leg hole of the underpants and kept banging into parked cars.

Finally he found the entrance.

So far so good, he thought.

He hopped over to the group of humans admiring the tropical butterflies and waited for them to notice him.

A horrible thought struck.

What if I've got the underpants on inside out? The colours won't look as bright. They'll think I'm just a drab moth.

He could feel something stabbing him in the forehead. He realised it wasn't anxiety, it was a label.

Everything was OK.

Then a man looked down.

Limpy flapped his arms inside the underpants. He did it slowly so he'd look like a butterfly who'd had a very busy day and was too tired to do any more actual flying.

The man saw him.

Limpy held his breath.

A wonderful thing happened. The man didn't chuck rocks at him or jump into a car and try to run him over.

It's working, thought Limpy delightedly.

Then the man's face went red.

'Arghhhh,' he yelled. 'A cane toad. In me undies.'

Other humans shouted and screamed.

The man lunged at Limpy.

Limpy leapt out of the underpants and flung himself at the fence. Luckily he was small enough to fit through the wire.

He hopped frantically across the carpark, trying to get over to a row of parked cars to hide underneath. To his horror he realised he was going too fast and his crook leg wasn't touching the ground properly and he was veering round in the beginnings of a circle.

The man was yelling behind him and the yells were getting closer.

Then Limpy saw that his circular hopping had brought him close to the big painted truck, which was revving its engine and starting to move off.

Limpy didn't hesitate.

He hopped higher than he'd ever hopped before and leapt onto the back of the truck and clung on to a brakelight with both hands and his good foot.

With a shuddering roar the truck surged forward into the sunset.

Limpy didn't look back.

He hung on with all his strength while the shouting behind him got fainter and fainter.

OK, he said to himself as he hurtled down the highway, I admit it. Pretending to be a butterfly was a dopey idea.

He sighed.

He should have taken one of the furry slippers and pretended to be a wombat.

* * *

The highway was soon dark but Limpy didn't mind because he knew exactly where he was going.

To the same place the truck was going, wherever that was.

A place where he could learn about disguises that actually worked. Disguises as good as the ones painted on the side of the truck.

Limpy hung on tight and had exciting visions of arriving back home with a pile of wonderful costumes. The cane toads would put them on and the humans driving on the highway would think the creatures in their headlights were echidnas and platypuses and kookaburras and butterflies and they'd drive past waving happily.

Suddenly the truck slowed down for a sharp bend in the highway.

Limpy realised it looked sort of familiar.

He peered around the back of the truck.

Ahead, lit up by the truck headlights

and an overhead light that also looked sort of familiar, was a railway crossing that looked very familiar.

And on the other side of it, sitting in the middle of the road, glaring at them and waving a stick, was a figure he recognised immediately.

Goliath.

The truck was accelerating over the crossing.

'Goliath,' yelled Limpy. 'Get out of the way.'

They were heading straight for him.

'Jump,' screamed Limpy. 'Jump to one side.'

Goliath jumped.

Too late.

The truck, with Limpy hanging onto the back frozen with horror, thundered over the top of Goliath.

'No!' cried Limpy.

He spun round, staring back at the circle of light on the road, desperately hoping to see Goliath still standing there waving his stick.

Or even tottering around, dazed.

Nothing.

Not even a blob of squashed skin

and warts.

Limpy turned back and put his anguished face against the back of the truck. Goliath must have been hit so hard he'd been pressed into the surface of the road.

Limpy felt sadness draining the strength out of his arms and his good leg. As the truck thundered into the night, one thought helped him hang on.

At least Charm hadn't been there.

This time.

By the next morning, Limpy was the world's biggest fan of brakelights.

Not only were they really useful to hang on to, but when you were spending a long night in the freezing slipstream at the back of a truck, they kept you alive.

Every time the truck hit its brakes, the brakelight bulb glowed and sent a beautiful burst of warmth through your aching body.

Mmmmm.

Except now that the sun was up and climbing fast, Limpy was starting to feel a bit too warm.

He was particularly worried about his armpits.

The problem with hanging onto a brakelight was that your armpits were exposed, and as the sun got higher, that could be a real problem.

Toast, thought Limpy anxiously. Fairly soon my pits'll be toast.

The brakelight came on again and stayed on for a long time while the truck slowed down.

Limpy felt himself overheating and becoming not quite such a big fan of brakelights.

Then he realised the truck was turning off the highway.

Phew, thought Limpy. At last. We're here.

The truck drove into a town.

Limpy knew it was a town because he'd seen photos of towns in the magazines people chucked out of cars.

The truck drove into the centre of the town and parked in a loading dock.

Limpy didn't know it was a loading dock because magazines don't have many photos of loading docks. All Limpy cared about was that he'd arrived at the place where he could get good disguises.

And then, thought Limpy happily, no more flat rellies.

He tensed.

The driver's door had just slammed and he could hear the driver coming round to the back of the truck.

Limpy let go of the brakelight and dropped to the floor.

His arms and legs were stiff and numb and he could hardly move, but he managed to hobble behind some trolleys.

Peering out he saw the driver fiddling with the back doors of the truck. A man in a suit appeared and pointed to his watch and pointed to his clipboard and said angry things to the driver. The driver scratched himself under his singlet and shrugged. He opened the truck doors and started lifting out big cardboard boxes. The man in the suit started opening the boxes.

Limpy stared.

Inside the boxes were huge numbers of small furry toys.

Limpy knew they were small furry toys because kids sometimes threw small furry toys out of cars, usually with sick on them.

Limpy gaped as the man in the suit

opened still more boxes.

These weren't just any small furry toys.

They were platypuses and echidnas and kookaburras.

Limpy wondered why humans were so keen on platypuses, echidnas and kookaburras. He'd met a few and they'd seemed pretty average. Nice enough, but nothing to paint a truck about.

Then Limpy noticed something else about the fluffy toys.

Not only did they not have sick on them, they were exactly the right size, if you pulled the stuffing out, for a cane toad to climb inside.

Perfect disguises.

Yes, thought Limpy ecstatically. All I've got to figure out now is how to get heaps of these toys back home without the man in the suit flattening me with his clipboard.

Limpy was still trying to figure out exactly how to do it when the driver suddenly came over and grabbed the trolley Limpy was hiding behind.

Limpy froze, desperately hoping the

driver wouldn't look down.

He didn't.

As soon as the driver had turned back to the truck, Limpy hurried out of the loading dock into the street.

The sun was so bright, Limpy was dazzled.

For a while he couldn't see a thing.

Then his eyes started working again and to his horror he found he was looking up at a circle of sneering human faces.

Teenagers.

He'd seen them in magazines, but rarely looking as cross as these ones.

'Yuk,' said one, 'a canie.'

'Let's get it,' said another.

Limpy didn't understand what they were saying.

He didn't need to.

The hands lunging at him and the feet swinging at him told him all he needed to know.

Ducking, weaving and hopping in a semi-circle, he managed to get across the footpath to the gutter. Ahead he saw the opening to a stormwater drain. Desperately hoping the teenagers wouldn't be able to squeeze in after him, he dived into it.

Limpy found himself sitting in a cool, dark tunnel with water trickling over his feet.

His skin started drinking in the water.

He told it to stop. There was no time for that. The angry faces of the teenagers were glaring down at him. They were kicking at the crumbling concrete, trying to make the opening to the drain bigger.

Limpy hopped for his life.

The tunnel was too narrow for him to hop in circles, so he was able to splash along at speed, bouncing from wall to wall.

He turned a corner, and then another, and the shouting of the kids faded into silence.

Not quite silence.

As he moved forward, Limpy could hear another sound above his head.

The buzz of other human voices.

Heaps of them.

Then the voices started cheering.

Limpy saw a shaft of light coming from another opening up ahead.

Weak with fear but tingling with curiosity, he climbed up the side of the drain and peered out.

He was under the main street of the town. Masses of humans were standing on both sides of the street grinning and cheering as if something wonderful was going to happen.

Limpy couldn't believe it. Surely this many humans wouldn't gather this quickly just to see a gang of teenagers trying to kill a cane toad?

Boy, humans really do hate us, he thought sadly.

Then the cheering got louder and the people started waving at something. Limpy saw what it was. An open-topped car, driving slowly along the street. Standing in it, waving to the crowd, was a girl wearing a sports singlet and holding a really long stick.

Limpy stared at the stick nervously.

He hoped it wasn't a special stick for poking down drains to stab cane toads.

Then the crowd started cheering even more loudly and Limpy saw something that made him forget even that horrible possibility.

In another open-topped car, following the girl's one, stood three figures he recognised.

A big platypus, a big echidna and a big kookaburra.

Not real ones. Three humans in costumes. Just like on the side of the truck.

The crowd was ecstatic. Limpy watched them cheering and whistling and blowing kisses to the kookaburra and the echidna and the platypus. Lots of the people were holding up the fluffy toys from the truck.

The whole town was in love with kookaburras, echidnas and platypuses.

Why? thought Limpy. What have they got that cane toads haven't? Apart from zips down their backs?

'Bloomin' show-offs,' said a voice next to his ear.

Limpy jumped, startled.

'Cloggin' up the whole town with their bloomin' parade,' said the voice.

Limpy saw that the voice belonged to a cockroach sitting next to him on the wall of the drain.

The cockroach saw Limpy and leapt back in alarm. Then its shiny brown shoulders slumped and it plodded towards Limpy with a weary sigh.

'I don't care,' it said morosely. 'Go on, eat me. What's the point of clingin' onto life down here in the sewers when mongrels like them up there get all the attention?'

'Don't worry,' said Limpy, 'I'm not going to eat you.' He meant it, even though he was ravenous. He needed information more than food. 'Those three up there,' he went on, 'why are they so popular with humans?'

'Games mascots, lucky buggers,' muttered the cockroach.

'Eh?' said Limpy. 'What do you mean, games?'

The cockroach gave him an incredulous look. 'What log have you been living under? The Games. Down south. Where humans from different countries do running and jumping against each other. Starts in a couple of days.'

'Oh, right,' pretended Limpy. 'The Games.'

He sort of knew what the cockroach was on about. Goliath and some of the kids at home used to have contests to see who could hop the fastest and who could fit the most slugs in their mouth. This sounded pretty similar.

'And what are mascots?' asked Limpy.

The cockroach rolled its eyes. 'Because there's heaps of humans coming from overseas for the Games, and millions more watching on telly, the organisers want to show them what a top place Australia is. So they've chosen three examples of our wildlife for everyone to go ga-ga over. Right now those mascots are the most popular individuals in Australia.' The cockroach looked sourly at the platypus, echidna and kookaburra. 'Beats me why they chose those three mangy losers.'

Limpy gazed up at the adoration on the faces of the humans as the mascots cruised slowly past.

One thing's for sure, he thought. Humans won't be driving over any platypuses, echidnas or kookaburras in the foreseeable future.

Suddenly Limpy knew what he had to do.

'Come on,' said the cockroach, 'get it over with. Eat me if you're going to.'

'I'm not going to,' said Limpy, as he watched the parade come to an end. 'Excuse me dashing, but I've got to make arrangements to be a Games mascot.'

Limpy hurried back along the stormwater drain, ideas bouncing around inside his head almost as fast as his body was bouncing around inside the tunnel.

The bloke with the clipboard who'd been yelling at the truck driver. He was obviously something to do with the Games. He looked pretty important.

I'll volunteer to him, thought Limpy happily. I'll tell him I'm available to be a Games mascot.

Limpy tingled with excitement.

Then he had a less happy thought.

What if the teenagers were waiting for him?

He had to take the risk. There was too much at stake. Once he was a Games mascot and humans adored him, he'd be able to introduce them to the family. And once people saw what kind, lovable, friendly folk Charm and the other cane toads were and how much fun you could have with them in mud pools, they'd stop trying to kill them.

Limpy bounced happily round a corner in the tunnel, and stopped dead.

Standing there sneering at him with narrow hate-filled eyes was the meanest-looking pack he'd ever seen.

Not teenagers.

Rats.

'So,' said the front rat, 'we heard we'd got a visitor.'

'G'day,' said Limpy nervously.

There were a lot of them.

'Excuse us if we seem rude,' said the rat, 'but we're going to skip the introductions and get straight on with ripping you to pieces.'

The rats advanced.

Limpy didn't hesitate.

He flexed his glands and sprayed streams of poisonous white pus over them.

It wasn't something he usually did to folk he'd only just met, but Mum was always reminding him to do it in emergencies, and this was certainly an emergency.

Limpy kept spraying till his poison glands were empty.

'Arghhh,' screamed the front rat, clawing at its face. 'That really hurts.'

The other rats were howling and rubbing their faces and backing away.

They turned and ran.

'Vicious mongrel,' yelled one as they went.

Limpy ignored that.

When his whole body had stopped shaking, he cautiously poked part of his head out of the drain opening and looked around.

No teenagers.

And there, in the loading dock, was the bloke with the clipboard.

As Limpy hurried across the footpath towards him, he saw that the bloke was still angry. Except this time it wasn't the driver he was angry at, it was the girl in the sports singlet who'd been holding the big stick in the parade.

She looked so unhappy, Limpy felt a pang of sympathy, even though Uncle

Bart had told him once it wasn't natural to feel sympathy for another species.

Limpy had never seen a human so miserable, not even kids in the backs of cars when the parents were playing their own music.

He hid behind a box in the loading dock, hoping something would happen to cheer the girl up.

'Why is it always me?' the girl was demanding, her dark pony-tail flapping angrily around her head. 'There are thousands of other athletes at the Games. Why can't you get one of them to appear at a dumb shopping centre for a change?'

'Because,' said the man, 'the public wants to see you. They don't want to see some ugly bloke in his twenties with a prickle haircut and lumpy legs. They want to see Australia's youngest and prettiest Games athlete.'

Limpy couldn't understand what the man was saying, but he could see the girl didn't like it. She threw her can of drink to the ground. The can rolled towards Limpy. It was another of the red ones with brown liquid trickling out of it.

'I'm an athlete, not a soapie star,' the girl said angrily. 'I've got training to do.'

'You're in great physical shape,' snapped the man. 'And if you stop drinking so much of that stuff, you'll stay that way.'

Suddenly the girl was in tears.

Limpy stared, sympathetic but fascinated. He'd heard about this weird thing humans could do with their eyes. Seeing it made him feel strange inside. Sort of sad.

'What would you know?' the girl was saying to the man through her tears. 'All you publicity people care about is ticket sales and TV ratings. You don't know anything about being an athlete.'

She ran off and the man banged his clipboard angrily against the truck and followed her.

Disappointed, Limpy watched the man go. So much for that plan. The man looked much too cross and distracted to be paying attention to Games mascot volunteers.

Limpy wondered where he could find a less angry Games official. It wouldn't be easy. He didn't know the first thing about the natural territory or feeding habits of Games officials.

Then he looked up at the truck and the answer popped into his mind.

A scary, dangerous answer.

But a good one.

Of course, thought Limpy. That's where Games officials must hang out. Down south, at the Games.

Limpy went over to the back of the truck and looked at the brakelight. He wondered how far away the Games were, and whether he could hang on to a lump of plastic for that long. Then he noticed some other passengers sitting on the rear number plate.

Two fruit flies.

'G'day,' said Limpy. 'Do you know if this truck's heading south to the Games?'

The fruit flies looked at Limpy nervously.

Limpy smiled at them and tried to look like a cane toad who'd just had a large lunch and wouldn't be eating any insects for several hours.

The fruit flies still looked nervous.

'We think it's heading south,' one said.

'We hope so,' said the other. 'We're planning to try our luck in the fruit industry down there.'

'Thanks,' said Limpy. 'Hope it goes well for you.'

At that moment a shadow fell over Limpy.

A big grinning human face appeared close to his.

Limpy realised why the fruit flies were still looking nervous.

The teenagers were back.

Limpy looked up at the grinning teenagers and hoped with all his strength that the truck would start up and head off for the Games so he could jump on the back and be whisked away.

It didn't.

One of the teenagers had a sweatshirt over his hands like a big glove.

With a sudden movement he picked Limpy up.

Limpy felt faint. He'd never been picked up before and he found he hated it even more than swamp spinach.

He kicked as hard as he could.

'Quit it,' said the teenager and started stroking Limpy's head.

Limpy stopped kicking. His warts began to tingle with—

He couldn't believe it.

Pleasure.

Suddenly he felt confused.

Perhaps he'd misjudged these particular humans.

The stroking continued and Limpy's whole body started to feel relaxed and sort of glowing. Perhaps, he thought dreamily, these fine humans work for a wildlife refuge at a petrol station and they've decided to add a cane toad to their collection and they've chosen me . . .

Except if they had, why was one of them taking the dust cap off one of the truck tyres?

'This'll be great,' sniggered the one with the dust cap. 'When you put compressed air in 'em they swell up like a balloon and explode.'

Limpy wished desperately that humans didn't have their own language. Why couldn't they speak normally like everyone else? Then he could understand what they were planning to do and decide if it was an emergency. He didn't want to be spraying poison around if it wasn't.

Limpy looked at the way the air-valve teenager was grinning cruelly at him. Then he felt something unpleasant between his legs. The one holding him had started fiddling with his bottom.

Limpy decided it was an emergency.

He flexed his glands and let them have it.

Except no poison came out.

Oh no, he remembered with a jolt of despair, I used it all up on the rats. My glands haven't refilled yet.

Limpy felt himself being lowered, bottom first, towards the air valve on the tyre. He tried to struggle and kick, but he was being held too tight. He closed his eyes and wished he was back at home in the swamp playing mud-slides with Charm. At least they could have a few more happy days together before she went food-collecting and a truck got her.

Suddenly another human voice rang out.

'Stop that!'

Limpy twisted round to see. It was the girl. She strode over and snatched him from the teenagers.

'Hey,' they shouted. 'Rack off, freak.'

Limpy, trembling with relief in her hands, was amazed at their stupidity. The girl was younger than them, but she was taller and her muscles were quite a bit bigger. Where he came from, if you were rude to someone with bigger muscles, you got eaten or at least heavily chewed.

The girl grabbed one of the teenagers by the ear and squeezed.

He squealed.

'You rack off,' she said.

Limpy saw the teenagers wondering whether to fight her.

She pulled out a mobile phone and started dialling.

The teenagers glanced at each other, then ran out of the loading dock and down the street.

'Freak,' they yelled back at the girl.

Limpy looked up at her. She was trembling too as she put the phone away.

He wished he could thank her, but he couldn't, so he just tried to look grateful.

'Come on,' she said. 'Let's get you back to your natural habitat.'

Limpy hoped she'd said, 'Let's get you back on the truck.'

He liked her face. It had freckles all over it, which, he decided, if she was a cane toad, would probably be the most beautiful warts.

Then he realised she wasn't putting him on the truck. She was carrying him across the street to a park.

'No,' he yelled. 'The truck. I've got to get on the truck.'

She didn't even look down.

This is hopeless, thought Limpy. She can't understand a word I'm saying.

That didn't stop him yelling all the way into the park.

'Poor thing,' she murmured. 'You're scared.'

Limpy didn't want to do what he did next, but this was an emergency.

He started kicking.

'Ow!' said the girl and put Limpy down on the grass.

He saw she was sucking her hand. He must have scratched her with his toenail. He wished he could say sorry, and thanks again, but he didn't have the language.

Or, he remembered in panic, the time.

Frantically he tried to hop back towards the loading dock, but just went round in circles.

The girl laughed, gave him a friendly wave, and left.

Oh well, he thought, at least I haven't hurt her.

Limpy forced himself to slow down. He hopped out of the park and back up the street, anxiously watching out for the teenagers.

As he got closer to the loading dock, he heard the one sound he didn't want to hear.

The truck engine revving.

'Wait,' he shouted as he hopped frantically towards the loading dock. 'Wait for me. Games mascot coming through. It's a matter of life and death.'

Just as he got to the loading dock entrance, the truck roared out into the street.

Limpy flung himself into the air and grabbed hold of the brakelight as it went past. He hung on, weak with relief, as the truck rumbled down the street.

The fruit flies, still sitting on the numberplate, looked at him nervously.

'Hello again,' said one. 'Are you going to try for a better life down south too?'

'Yes,' panted Limpy. 'You could say that.'

The worst part of the trip wasn't the sun, even though it blazed down onto the back of the truck all afternoon and Limpy was soon feeling like one of those oven-baked crinkle-cut chips, the burnt ones that humans were always tossing out of cars.

This is ridiculous, he thought weakly. They'll never let me be a Games mascot if I'm cooked.

Then he had an idea.

Slowly, painfully, he eased himself away from the brakelight and down towards the rear bumper bar. All he had to hang onto were the rivets holding the truck together. He gripped them with both hands and his good foot to stop himself being blown away by the slipstream or jolted onto the highway each time the truck hit a pothole. Finally, he slid in behind the bumper bar. He was blistered and bruised, and the metal bumper bar was hot, but at least he was in the shade.

The worst part of the trip wasn't the fruit flies either, even though they joined Limpy behind the bumper bar and wouldn't stop yakking about fruit.

'Plums,' said one. 'You can't beat a good Queen Victoria.'

'How would you know?' said the other. 'When have you had a plum?'

'Don't need to. I can tell from the look.'

'Bull. Apples are better than plums any day!'

'Get lost, you've never even seen an apple.'

'Have so. Beautiful orange colour. Long and thin. Green foliage growing out the top.'

Limpy sighed.

He was very hungry and even though two fruit flies wouldn't make much difference to the emptiness in his stomach, he was very tempted.

He resisted the temptation. They were all bouncing southwards on the same truck, and it just didn't seem right to be eating folk you were sharing an adventure with.

The worst part of the trip came after the sun had set and the bumper bar had cooled down and the fruit flies had fallen asleep and there was a blissful silence except for the rumble of the tyres on the highway and the bumping and squeaking of the rear suspension.

As they sped through the last of the sub-tropical flatlands, Limpy heard faint sounds in the distance that made his warts prickle.

Cane toads, calling to each other in the dusk.

Limpy listened to the far-off voices arguing about whether stink beetles were better-looking insects than meat maggots, and felt a sudden pang of loneliness.

He thought about Mum and Dad and hoped they weren't worrying about him too much.

He thought about Charm and hoped she was staying away from the road.

He thought about Goliath, and even though he'd never had that much in common with Goliath, specially Goliath's favourite game of swallowing mud worms and placing bets on which one would crawl out of his bottom first, Limpy realised he missed him.

Limpy listened again to the voices of the distant cane toads and thought about his hundreds of brothers and sisters. He hadn't seen any of them since they were tadpoles and a rainstorm had swept them all away, leaving only him and Charm.

Some of them could be out there now, thought Limpy, arguing about whether a slimy lugworm tasted better than a shovel-nosed centipede.

He was doing this for them as well.

Even as he had the thought, another pang shot through him.

It was partly love, but mostly hunger.

Suddenly Limpy felt weak and dizzy from lack of food. He couldn't remember the last time he'd eaten. He stuck his head over the rim of the bumper bar. The air was rushing past much too quickly for even the lightning-fast tongue of a cane toad to pluck insects out of it.

His empty stomach sank as he realised what he must do.

Go to the front of the truck.

* * *

It took half the night.

Luckily there were rivets along the side of the truck for Limpy to cling to, but his progress was painfully slow. The air was ripping past so fast and the truck was bouncing so much that he could only go forward in tiny, sliding movements.

Several times he slipped and the black howling highway rushed up at him, but somehow he managed to hang on and drag himself back.

Several other times waves of tiredness and hunger swept through him and he felt like just letting go and sleeping forever. Except he knew he wouldn't just be sleeping, he'd be smeared over half a kilometre of highway and having nightmares for years to come as his family got flattened.

Finally, with a last desperate effort,

Limpy dragged himself around the driver's-side door hinge, across the front wheel arch and onto the bullbar.

He blinked in the glare from the headlights.

It was better than he'd dared hope.

There were insects everywhere. Grasshoppers, mosquitos, locusts, beetles, midges, moths, gnats, flying ants, cicadas, all splattered across the front of the truck in a juicy, mouth-watering smorgasbord.

Limpy ate like he'd never eaten before.

He'd have eaten even faster if the air hadn't been battering against him so hard that he had to hang on with at least one hand and his good foot.

Then he discovered that if he turned round to face the onrushing air and just opened his mouth, an endless stream of insects were flung into it.

Weak with relief, he let himself be filled.

It wasn't till afterwards he realised that what happened next probably saved him from exploding, or at least getting a serious tummy ache.

At first he thought he was hearing things, but when he listened more carefully he knew he wasn't.

It was definitely a voice, feebly calling out.

'Limpy. Help.'

A voice he recognised.

Limpy nearly fell off the bullbar in shock.

It couldn't be.

Goliath?

'Limpy,' croaked Goliath's voice. 'Down here.'

Limpy clambered frantically across the bullbar, heart thudding louder than the tyres, trying to hear if it really was Goliath, straining to catch a glimpse of him.

How could it be after Goliath had been flattened by the same speeding ten-wheeler Limpy was clinging to the front of now?

Squinting in the glare of the headlights, Limpy searched the radiator grille, the indicator housings, even the fog-light brackets.

No Goliath.

I must be hearing things, thought Limpy. I've overstressed my digestive system and my blood's rushing to my stomach and starving my brain.

'Limpy,' wheezed the voice. 'Underneath.'

For a second Limpy thought the voice meant underneath the fog-light bracket, but he quickly realised that couldn't be it. There wasn't even enough room under a fog-light bracket for a fruit fly on a vegetable juice diet.

Limpy realised the voice meant underneath the truck.

He wrapped his arms round the bottom rung of the bullbar and peered down between the front wheels.

And gasped.

There, wedged between the front axle cover and the main chassis of the truck, smeared with oil, covered in dust and spitting road gravel out through dry lips, was Goliath.

Limpy blinked and swung his head round to use his other eye, just in case he was seeing things.

He wasn't.

'Goliath,' yelled Limpy. 'Are you OK?'

'No,' croaked Goliath, 'I'm not. I'm a hit-and-run victim.'

Limpy decided not to point out that

hit-and-run victims didn't usually threaten trucks with sticks.

'I've been yelling for ages,' complained Goliath, 'but you were more interested in hanging off the side of the truck.'

'Sorry,' said Limpy. 'Are you hurt?'

Goliath didn't answer.

Limpy didn't like the look of him. The way his arms and legs were just hanging loose and his face was pushed into his own bottom. He could have broken bones and internal injuries.

'Help me out of here,' croaked Goliath. 'I'm gunna rip this bloke's doors off and shove his engine up his nose.'

Then again, perhaps not.

Limpy scraped a handful of grasshopper bits off the radiator grille and swung himself under the front of the truck.

The roadway hissed past his head, hungry for his brains.

Limpy ignored it.

Upside down, careful to keep his crook leg off the road, he clambered across to Goliath.

‘Hang on,’ he said.

‘Don’t need to,’ said Goliath gloomily. ‘It’ll take a crowbar to get me out of here.’

Limpy swung onto the axle cover next to his cousin. For a skinny cane toad there was plenty of room. Now he was close, Limpy winced. For a cane toad the size of Goliath it was a tragically tight fit.

Limpy moistened Goliath’s lips with grasshopper juice, then fed him the bits.

Goliath gulped them down.

‘Thanks,’ he said. ‘Hey, what are you doing?’

‘Lubrication,’ said Limpy, scooping up handfuls of truck oil from the axle cover and rubbing them into Goliath’s warty skin. ‘It’s a concept I learned from a slug.’

When Goliath was covered with oil, Limpy clambered round to the other side of the axle and started pushing.

Goliath didn’t budge.

Limpy braced himself against a brake fluid hose and pushed till his warts felt like they’d pop.

Still Goliath didn't shift.

This is hopeless, thought Limpy. I'll have to starve him till he gets thin. Which could take weeks. Meanwhile, if a rock flies up from the road . . .

Then Limpy remembered something.

Goliath was scared of dust mites.

Giant lizards didn't fluster him a bit, enraged funnel-web spiders usually copped an earful if they tried it on with Goliath, but dust mites sent him into a panic.

Limpy took a deep breath. It was risky, but he didn't have any choice.

'Sorry I'm not pushing very hard,' he said in a loud voice behind Goliath. 'I keep slipping on all the dust mites.'

Goliath gave a scream louder than all the air brakes going on at once, and disappeared.

Limpy stared around in panic.

Oh no, Goliath must have wrenched himself free and leapt straight onto the road.

I shouldn't have done it, thought Limpy, distraught. I should have just tickled him.

Then he saw something moving up ahead.

Something large and hanging upside down from the truck chassis.

It was Goliath, wide-eyed with terror, scrabbling his way towards the front of the truck.

By the time Limpy caught up, Goliath was on the bullbar gobbling insect fragments. Now that he had a mouthful of grasshopper, locust, midge, moth, gnat and cicada, he seemed to have forgotten about the dust mites.

Limpy showed him how to turn round and get a fresh supply of dinner.

After a very long time, Goliath burped and gave Limpy a grin. Limpy beamed back. His crook leg was twitching with happiness to see Goliath. He gave Goliath a delighted punch on the arm. Goliath gave him a slap on the back that nearly knocked him off the truck.

'Thanks old mate,' said Goliath. He glared up at the driver's cabin. 'Now I'm gunna teach this mongrel a lesson, starting with ripping his wheels off and peeing in his fuel tank.'

'Actually,' said Limpy, 'I'd like this truck to get to where it's going.'

He told Goliath about the Games and being a mascot.

Goliath stared at him. 'Have you been frying your brains in the sun?'

Limpy sighed. New ideas always took a while to sink in with Goliath.

'We'll both be frying our brains in the sun if we stay out here much longer,' said Limpy. 'Come on, follow me.'

He led Goliath across the wheel arch and over the door hinge to the side of the truck. Halfway along was a rip in the aluminium cladding he'd spotted earlier where the truck must have scraped something.

It was just big enough for Limpy to squeeze through.

Goliath was another matter, but thanks to the axle grease on his skin, and after a lot of hard work by Limpy, he flopped through too.

They looked around at the boxes of fluffy toys.

'This'll be us once I'm a mascot,' said

Limpy happily. 'Fluffy cane toads, and humans going gaga over us.

Goliath stared at him again. 'Limpy,' he said, 'do you know how much competition there is to be a Games mascot? I met a spider under the truck who'd travelled across the country to be one and it didn't even get an audition.'

Limpy felt his spirits droop.

'Gee,' he said. 'It must have been disappointed.'

Goliath frowned and thought about this. 'Possibly,' he said. 'I forgot to ask before I swallowed it.'

Limpy stared at the fluffy toys, his glands heavy with worry.

Then he had a thought that made him tingle with relief.

'Must have been a furry spider,' he said.

Goliath looked impressed. 'Yeah,' he said. 'It tickled as it went down. How did you know?'

'That's why it didn't get the job,' said Limpy happily. 'There's already a mascot with fur, and one with feathers, and one with spikes. But not one with warts. Not yet.'

'Good thought,' said Goliath. He sat pondering for a while, then he broke into a grin. 'Here's another good thought,' he said. 'When we get down south, let's find some humans and stuff these fluffy toys up the mongrels' exhaust pipes so their cars blow up.'

Limpy sighed.

He decided not to ask Goliath if he wanted to be a mascot too.

The air brakes squealed on and Limpy found himself rolling across the floor in a flock of fluffy echidnas.

He sat up and listened.

The truck had stopped moving. It gave a shudder as the engine died.

'I think we've arrived,' said Limpy.

'Water,' croaked Goliath. 'Slime. Anything.'

Limpy went over and pulled a handful of fluff out of Goliath's mouth.

'It doesn't help,' said Limpy, 'when you try and eat a brushed-polyester platypus.'

'I thought it might have some moisture in it,' croaked Goliath.

Limpy knew how he felt. They'd been in the back of the truck for a whole day without a drop of liquid. Since early morning, all Limpy had been thinking about was a drink. He'd have drunk anything. Which is why he was so glad Goliath hadn't done a pee.

A loud clang echoed through the truck.

'Arghh!' yelled Goliath. 'What's that?'

'They're opening the doors,' said Limpy. 'Quick, before they find us.'

He pushed Goliath through the hole in the side of the truck and squeezed through himself. As he dropped onto the road, a barrage of sights and sounds hit him.

Traffic everywhere.

Humans all over the place.

The night sky almost as bright as day.

Limpy huddled with Goliath under the truck and tried to take it all in.

Stack me, he thought, so this is a city.

He'd seen pictures of cities on beer cartons, but he had no idea they were so noisy. Or smelly. He could smell car fumes and animals cooking and a hundred other weird aromas. One of them, he thought with a shudder, could easily be the stuff he'd heard humans sprayed on their armpits.

'This is scary,' Goliath was saying, looking around wide-eyed.

Limpy knew how he felt. There were roads going in all directions with millions of cars and trucks on them. No wonder cane toads didn't live in cities. They wouldn't stand a chance.

'I'm staying here,' said Goliath, stepping further back under the truck.

Then Limpy smelt something else.

Water.

He pointed to a large round building across a busy road.

'I think there's water in there,' said Limpy.

Goliath lunged forward.

Limpy grabbed onto him and tried to stop him crashing into cars and colliding with humans in his desperation to get across the road.

But once they'd hopped frantically between the vehicles, and scampered into the concrete tunnel that led into the building, the smell of water was so strong that Limpy let himself be dragged along.

He closed his eyes for a moment and pretended that at the other end of the tunnel was his own swamp, with Mum and Dad and Charm waiting to hug him and tell him that everything was OK because all humans had decided to stop driving and stay in and watch telly forever.

Limpy knew it wouldn't be and they hadn't, but it felt good just for a moment.

What actually happened was almost as good.

He and Goliath burst out of the tunnel into a huge open space. Lights shimmered in the night sky. Grass glistened. The air sparkled.

'It's raining!' yelled Goliath and flung himself into the cascade of shimmering droplets.

Limpy did the same. He felt his fear and stress start to trickle away with the water that ran blissfully over his parched skin.

Maybe cities aren't so bad, he thought, if all the big buildings have paddocks in them, and rain.

But even as he drank in the delicious

water, he noticed something strange about the rain.

It wasn't falling from the sky, it was spurting up out of the grass.

Stack me, thought Limpy, no wonder humans up our way frown when it rains. They must be really confused seeing it dropping out of the sky.

Limpy didn't care where it came from.

He drank and drank.

After a while he was vaguely aware that Goliath had stopped drinking and grunting happily, and was stretching his big muscles and saying something like 'back in a sec'.

Limpy had been deep in thought about how he'd try and learn human language once he was a Games mascot so he could explain to them about rain. He looked up and saw Goliath striding off across the oval.

'Where are you going?' he called.

'Revenge,' replied Goliath.

Limpy leapt up in alarm.

Which is when he saw, at the far end of the oval, a lone human figure in a sports singlet doing warm-up exercises.

Limpy peered through the rain.

There was something familiar about the human. Its dark hair was in a ponytail and when Limpy squinted he was sure he could see freckles on its face. But it wasn't till it picked up a very long stick that Limpy recognised her.

'Wait, Goliath,' he yelled. 'Don't hurt her. She's the one who rescued me.'

Goliath didn't hear. He strode on towards the girl, his shoulders hunched like they always were when he boasted how one day he'd bash up a human.

Limpy hurried after him.

Just before Goliath reached the girl she suddenly held the stick over her head, sprinted for a while, then jammed one end of the stick into the ground and pivoted herself with it high into the air.

Very high.

Limpy gaped.

He'd seen creatures with some pretty spectacular ways of escaping predators, but nothing like this.

He watched the girl turn gracefully in the air, then plummet down onto what looked like a very large car-seat cushion. By the time she sat up, Goliath was next to her, grabbing at her stick where it had fallen.

Spectacular, thought Limpy anxiously, but not that effective with predators who were maniacs.

'Goliath,' he yelled, hurrying over. 'Don't.'

'I'm gunna whack her one with this,' said Goliath, muscles and eyes bulging as he tried to pick up the stick. It didn't budge.

The girl looked over and saw Goliath. Her eyes bulged too, in amazement.

'A cane toad?' she said. 'You're a bit far south, aren't you?'

Goliath glared at her.

Limpy flung himself forward. Suddenly he didn't know if he was trying to rescue Goliath or the girl. Then he realised it didn't matter because he was going round in circles.

The girl saw him.

Her mouth fell open. She stared for a long time.

'Don't I know you?' she said at last.

Limpy didn't understand what she was saying, but he hoped she was pleased to see him.

The girl looked over to where the truck was being noisily unloaded at the edge of the stadium.

'Stack me,' she said. 'Did you hitch a ride?'

Limpy still couldn't understand, but the sparkle in her eyes and the size of her grin gave him hope, and then a brilliant idea.

Perhaps she could help him apply to be a mascot. If he could just find a way of asking.

Behind her, he saw, on a post holding up a roof over a hillside covered in seats, was a big picture of the other mascots. Limpy went over to it, hopped up and clung to the picture so he was between the kookaburra and the platypus.

He waited for the girl to understand.

He could see she was thinking hard.

Finally she spoke. 'I'm really glad to see you guys,' she said. 'You can be a big help to me tomorrow.'

Limpy was pretty sure he

understood. 'Yes,' he was pretty sure she'd said, 'I can definitely help you apply to be a mascot.'

So, unlike Goliath, he wasn't at all worried when she picked them both up and put them in her sports bag.

'Yum,' said Goliath, 'shoes.'

Limpy sighed.

He took a deep breath and tried to explain to Goliath that when a person has let you spend the night in her bath at the Games village, and shared her mushrooms on toast with you, and let you sit up late watching telly with her, and is now taking you in her bag to meet the Games Mascot Committee, it's pretty ungrateful to eat her shoes.

Goliath spat out a lace and thought about this.

'You're right,' he said after a bit. 'I'll eat her socks.'

Limpy was about to snatch the sock from him when the bag tilted violently and they both went sprawling into a damp towel.

From the way the bag was moving,

Limpy guessed the girl was carrying them up some steps.

The Games Mascot Committee is probably so important, he thought, they have their meetings up on a roof where snakes can't get them.

He'd seen the committee on telly the night before. They'd certainly looked important, sitting behind a long table showing off kookaburra pencil cases and echidna bathmats and platypus car-seat covers to a big crowd of people with cameras and notebooks.

Limpy felt his warts tingling with excitement. He hoped when he met the committee his mouth didn't get so dry with nervousness that his mucus dried up. Mum always reckoned a cane toad didn't look his best unless he had a bit of mucus on his lips.

Suddenly Limpy heard the muffled sound of applause and the chatter of human voices and the clicking of cameras.

He felt the girl unzip the bag.

Stack me, he thought. She must be going to introduce me to the Mascot Committee in front of the people with the cameras and notebooks.

Limpy hurriedly practised his smile. He needed one that would win the hearts of humans everywhere. It wasn't easy in a dark bag without a swamp to check your reflection in.

Then suddenly the bag wasn't dark any more. The girl had opened it and was reaching in. Heart thumping, Limpy pushed himself towards her groping hand.

But her hand slid past him and grabbed Goliath.

'Uh?' grunted Goliath, spitting out a mouthful of towel.

Limpy watched in horror as the girl lifted Goliath out of the bag. Through the open zip he could see lights on tall poles and human faces gawking. On a stage the girl held Goliath close to her cheek and smiled sweetly at the cameras.

Please, Limpy begged Goliath silently. Don't blow it. Don't attack anyone with a stick. Not today.

Limpy's view out of the bag was suddenly blocked by a human body. Limpy stood on tiptoe and saw it was the bloke in the suit with the clipboard. He was looking cross as usual, and trying to grab Goliath from the girl.

He and the girl said some angry things to each other.

Limpy couldn't see a Games Mascot Committee anywhere.

The bloke was pulling Goliath's legs. The girl was hanging onto his arms. 'Hey,' yelled Goliath indignantly. 'Take it easy. Watch my back.'

Limpy was about to leap out of the bag and try and explain to them that just because Goliath looked tough, that didn't mean he was made of steel-belted rubber.

Then the bag began to fall.

Limpy hung onto the towel but it didn't do any good.

The bag hit the ground with a thud and Limpy's head bashed into his knee and suddenly he was out in the glaring lights, skidding across a shiny surface.

'Help,' he yelled. 'New mascot over here.'

Nobody heard him, and when he stopped sliding and his head stopped spinning he realised why. The bag had fallen off the back of the stage and he was lying among some plastic pot plants out of sight of the crowd.

In the distance, he could hear the girl and the clipboard bloke still arguing. And another voice, much closer.

'Fog,' it said.

Limpy looked up.

A human toddler in a nappy and a T-shirt was looking down at him, wide-eyed.

Oh no, thought Limpy. That's all I need. A kid getting terrified and everyone blaming me. I'll never get to be a mascot if they think I'm cruel to kids.

'It's OK,' he said to the toddler. 'I'm not going to hurt you.'

The toddler grinned, dropped the teddy bear it was holding by one leg, grabbed Limpy's leg, and toddled off, dragging Limpy behind it.

'Fog,' chortled the toddler.

Limpy sighed.

He resisted the temptation to give the toddler a tiny little spray.

Instead, as he was sliding along on

his back, he looked around.

He was in a huge space, almost as big as the stadium but with a roof. There were shops everywhere, on lots of different levels. It didn't look like the committee meeting place he'd seen on telly.

Why did she bring us here, Limpy wondered, if it wasn't to meet the Games Mascot Committee?

He didn't understand.

As the toddler dragged him into a shop, Limpy waited anxiously for the girl to come and rescue him again.

A thought nagged at him.

What had his Uncle Preston's last words been? The ones he'd said just before he was flattened by a funeral procession?

That's right.

'Never trust a human.'

'Yuk,' said Goliath, 'toothpaste.'

Limpy sighed.

He took a deep breath and tried to explain to Goliath that when a young athlete has paid a lot of money to a shopping-centre security guard for your freedom and then smuggled you back to the Games village in her bag and hidden you under her bed so an angry bloke with a clipboard can't get his hands on you, it's pretty ungrateful to eat her antiseptic foot cream.

Goliath spat out a band-aid and thought about this.

'Why should we be grateful?' he said. 'She was meant to be taking us to meet the Games Mascot Committee and all we ended up with was sore backs.'

'It wasn't all bad,' said Limpy. 'That shop the toddler dragged me into was full of tellies. I was there for ages before the security guard found me. You can learn a lot of useful stuff about humans from telly, even if you don't speak their language. Did you know there's a very famous person on telly named after one of our dead uncles?'

'Who?' said Goliath. 'Roly?'

'No,' said Limpy. 'Bart.'

Goliath looked impressed. He stopped eating the stuff in the bag. Limpy took the foot cream away from him in case he got hungry again.

'But she still didn't take us to the committee,' said Goliath, 'did she?'

Limpy sighed again.

Goliath was right.

Why hadn't she?

Limpy was still puzzling it over when the bag was slid out from under the bed. The girl lifted him and Goliath out and offered them dinner.

'Here,' she said. 'I got you these from the carpark.'

Limpy wasn't hungry, not even for the radiator-grilled grasshoppers she held out to him.

Then he noticed the telly was on and

saw what was on the screen. The girl and the clipboard bloke fighting over Goliath at the shopping centre.

'That's me,' yelled Goliath through a mouthful of grasshopper.

Limpy stared.

Not at his cousin being stretched on the screen. At the expression on the girl's face in the room now as she watched. Everyone on the screen looked angry or shocked or upset, including Goliath. But the girl's expression now, as she watched the chaos, was delighted, gleeful, ecstatic.

Suddenly Limpy understood.

She'd planned the whole thing. She'd taken him and Goliath to the shopping centre on purpose to upset the bloke with the clipboard. To pay him back, probably for making her do something she didn't want to do.

She hadn't been doing them a favour, they'd been doing her one.

Boy, thought Limpy, perhaps Uncle Preston was right about not trusting humans.

The shopping centre bit finished on the telly and Limpy saw the girl smiling down at him fondly. She didn't look selfish or dishonest. She just looked like a friendly human who'd rescued him twice.

Then Limpy realised what must have happened.

Of course, he thought. She didn't trick us, she just hasn't understood. She hasn't got it. She hasn't grasped that I want to be a mascot.

On a shelf above the telly, Limpy saw, was a set of the fluffy mascot toys.

He decided it was worth one more try.

He hopped up onto the shelf and sat between the platypus and the echidna, trying to look as much as possible like a mascot.

The girl laughed, lifted him back down and offered him another grasshopper.

'Give up,' mumbled Goliath with his mouth full.

Limpy ignored him, hopped back up and took his position again with the other mascots.

This time the girl didn't laugh.

She stared at him and the other

mascots for a long time, frowning.

I think she's getting it, thought Limpy. I think she understands.

He decided she was.

What was it Uncle Roly had been saying just before he was flattened by that caravan?

'Life's a long hard journey, young Limpy,' he'd said. 'But you'll get more out of it if you look on the bright side.'

Limpy looked on the bright side for the rest of that evening, and all night in front of the telly, and most of the next morning, right up until the girl put him and Goliath back into her bag, put the bag back under the bed, and left without them.

Limpy managed to open the bag zip from the inside and scramble out from under the bed just in time to hear a vehicle driving off.

'What's happening?' said Goliath, appearing next to Limpy with a mouthful of sock fluff.

'She's left us behind,' said Limpy, numb with disappointment.

Goliath thought about this.

'Perhaps she's just gone to get some more grasshoppers,' he said. 'Or socks.'

'Nah,' said a voice.

Limpy looked up. Sitting on the bedspread was a mosquito.

'She's gone to the opening,' said the mosquito.

'What opening?' said Limpy. He thought of all the openings he'd seen on telly. Garage doors. Cats' mouths. Tubs of yoghurt. The openings humans got in them when they were shot.

'The Games,' said the mosquito. 'Opening ceremony. Big event. All the athletes'll be there. Huge crowd. Top feed.'

The mosquito sighed wistfully.

Limpy sighed mournfully. He couldn't believe it. She still hadn't understood. Here they were, a human and a cane toad who actually cared about each other, and he couldn't get one simple idea across to her.

It's hopeless, thought Limpy, crook leg aching with despair. I give up.

Who had he been kidding? How could one slightly squashed cane toad hope to change things that had been going on since the dawn of time?

Limpy opened his mouth to tell Goliath they were going home.

Before he could, the mosquito sighed again. 'Makes me hungry just thinking about it, a feed like that.'

Limpy found himself thinking of Charm and what she'd be doing when she got hungry. Going down to the highway and having a feed there. A tiny target, fixed in the headlights.

Suddenly his warts prickled with determination.

I won't give up, he thought. I can't.

Limpy saw that he and the mosquito weren't the only ones thinking about food. Goliath was climbing up the bedspread and was almost close enough to reach the mosquito with his tongue.

Limpy hauled on Goliath's leg with all his strength.

Goliath crashed to the floor.

'Ow,' he yelled.

Limpy gave him a glare.

The mosquito was buzzing nervously.

'Don't fly off,' said Limpy. 'I promise my cousin won't do that again. He'd forgotten we're trying to save our species from extinction and we need your help.'

'Funny way of showing it,' said the mosquito.

'Sorry,' mumbled Goliath.

'The Games opening,' said Limpy to the mosquito. 'Will the mascots be there?'

'Will they ever,' said the mosquito. 'Biggest day for the mascots. They wouldn't miss it. Not with millions of people watching on telly.'

Limpy felt his glands tingle with excitement.

'And,' he said, 'are you going to the opening?'

'Nah,' said the mosquito sadly. 'Too windy. Take me a week to get there.'

'We could give you a ride,' said Limpy. 'You could hop on my back and hang on to a wart.'

The mosquito looked doubtfully at Goliath.

'Don't worry about me,' said Goliath. 'I'm full. I've eaten a sock.'

The mosquito buzzed down and landed on Limpy's back.

'Great,' said Limpy. 'Now, I'm OK till we get out the bathroom window, but after that you'll have to give me directions.'

*   *   *

Limpy stuck his head up out of the stormwater drain in the middle of the stadium and nearly fainted with shock.

He'd never seen so many humans.

The stadium was full of them.

Humans in tracksuits.

Humans in blazers.

Humans in security-guard uniforms.

Marching. Waving huge flags. Directing crowds.

And behind them, towering into the sky on all sides, vast paddocks of seated humans cheering and waving small fluffy mascots and throwing streamers at the parade.

The whole spectacle was noisier than a truckload of chooks going over a railway crossing.

A hundred truck-loads.

Stack me, thought Limpy, I didn't know there were this many humans in the whole world, including Tasmania.

'Yum,' said the mosquito. 'Just as

well I'm hungry.'

Limpy saw that Goliath was looking pretty stunned too, and Goliath was used to big crowds because sometimes when he got hungry he just stuck his head into a termite's nest. He was looking like he wished he had his head in one now.

'Limpy,' said Goliath nervously. 'I don't reckon we should be here.'

'Relax,' said Limpy, trying to ignore his pounding heart and the roaring crowd. 'This is exactly where we should be.'

He peered around, trying to spot the mascots.

At first he couldn't see them among all the athletes and officials and security guards and TV cameras.

Then the mosquito pointed and Limpy looked up and there they were, huge on a giant screen at one end of the stadium, the kookaburra and the platypus and the echidna, waving to the crowd from the back of a massive fake rock on wheels.

Limpy looked around the stadium again and saw the rock at the head of the parade, surrounded by TV cameras, trundling slowly towards him along the running track.

He decided not to risk leaving Goliath on his own. No point winning the hearts and minds of the human race if your cousin was nearby threatening them with sticks.

'Thanks for your help,' Limpy said to the mosquito. He turned to Goliath. 'Come on.'

Limpy set off towards the running track, desperately trying not to hop in circles or get crushed by human feet. Shoes, boots, trainers, sandals and thongs thudded down, sometimes a flea's whisker from his head.

Please, begged Limpy silently. I survived being hit by a truck, please don't let my quest be ended now by a tennis shoe.

Limpy reached the running track with just enough time to glance back, drag Goliath out from under a TV cable and leap for the float.

He clambered up the side of the rock, Goliath at his side.

'OK,' he said to Goliath when they

were at the top between the kookaburra and the platypus. 'You're a mascot. Look appealing.'

Goliath looked puzzled.

Limpy sighed, then turned to the crowd and smiled and waved.

He hoped the other mascots wouldn't mind. Luckily they were too tall to have noticed yet, but they would once the crowd started cheering for the cane toads.

Which they weren't doing so far.

Not even now that Goliath was smiling and waving too.

We're too small, thought Limpy in despair. The crowd can't see us.

He was about to climb onto Goliath's shoulders when the crowd started making a different noise.

Suddenly, instead of cheering, they were booing and making strange gurgles in their throats. It sounded to Limpy like a stadium full of humans about to be sick.

Then he saw himself, huge, on the giant screen.

Which is where all the humans were looking.

Limpy felt cold dread seep through his glands.

'Smile,' said a cheery voice. 'You're on telly.'

The mosquito, buzzing overhead, was pointing to a nearby TV camera that was pointing at Limpy.

'What's happening?' said Limpy. 'Why are the crowd making that noise?'

The mosquito rolled its eyes. 'Why do you think?'

Goliath took a menacing step towards the mosquito, which made Goliath appear on the big screen too.

The crowd made even louder gagging noises.

'Answer the question,' said Goliath.

'Well,' said the mosquito, choosing his words carefully, 'it's because humans think cane toads are the ugliest, most revolting-looking creatures they've ever seen.'

Limpy struggled to digest this.

'They think you're even uglier and more revolting,' said the mosquito, 'than hairy spiders and smelly dung beetles and those slugs that sleep in their own snot.'

Limpy looked around the stadium at all the humans gazing up at the screen pretending to stick their fingers down their throats.

He could understand them doing that if it was just him up there with his crook leg. But Goliath, the handsomest cane toad he'd ever seen, was up there too.

It must be true.

Limpy felt sick himself.

It's hopeless, he thought miserably. Nobody wants a revolting mascot. I'll never win the hearts and minds of humans now. They'll carry on hating us and killing us forever.

Limpy turned away so he wouldn't have to see the revulsion and hatred on the faces of the crowd.

And found himself staring at the revulsion and hatred on the faces of the security guards advancing towards him.

For a fleeting moment Limpy was tempted to let the security guards grab him.

What did it matter now if he was arrested and locked up for impersonating a Games mascot and making a stadium full of humans feel sick?

Now I know the truth, thought Limpy miserably, I might as well rot in a human jail for all the good I can do anyone.

Then he saw what was happening to Goliath.

Goliath was hopping from side to side on the rock, dodging blows from the kookaburra mascot who'd taken off his kookaburra head and was trying to bash Goliath with the big plastic beak. The rock, which was also made of plastic, was splintering under the blows. Goliath's poison glands were bulging with fury.

'No,' Limpy yelled at Goliath. 'Don't.'

He threw himself at his cousin and they both tumbled off the rock and crashed down onto the running track.

Goliath yelped with surprise and pain.

'What are you doing?' he protested. 'You're meant to be on my side.'

'The security guards have got guns,' panted Limpy. 'They'll use them if you fire first.'

Goliath sighed. 'Spoilsport!' he muttered.

As Limpy dragged himself out from under the complaining Goliath, he saw that the boots of the nearest security guard were getting very close.

Slightly closer, but only just, was the entrance to a stormwater drain.

'Hop for it!' yelled Limpy.

He pushed Goliath towards the drain, and together they scrambled into it with the dust from the security guards' boots stinging their backs.

‘Let me spray the mongrels,’ panted Goliath. ‘Please. Just a quick one up their trouser legs.’

‘No,’ said Limpy. ‘Keep moving.’

But after they’d splashed along the drain only a short distance, Limpy suddenly couldn’t keep moving himself. Suddenly his body felt too heavy with despair to take another step.

‘If you’re stopping, I’m stopping,’ said Goliath, sitting down heavily in the trickle of water.

Limpy hardly noticed.

All he could hear was the distant sound of the jeering humans in the stadium.

Millions of humans, all thinking him and Goliath and Mum and Dad and Charm were ugly and revolting. Mum with her kind smile and beautiful yellow eyes. Dad with his sense of humour and the funny tricks he could do with mucus. Charm with her gorgeous warty eyelids and her loving nature and the cute way the corners of her mouth crinkled when she was eating a mouse.

I was the only one who could save

them, thought Limpy miserably, and I've failed.

Even now, huge trucks could be thundering down the wrong side of the highway, aiming straight for them.

And station wagons towing huge caravans.

And buses full of fat toddlers.

Limpy wished his eyes could do that wet thing that humans' eyes did. It seemed to help them when they were full of misery and despair.

All he could do was sit there, aching.

'Pssst.'

Limpy looked up, thinking Goliath's poison was leaking.

It wasn't.

A large slug was beckoning to them from further along the drain.

'Move yourselves,' said the slug. 'You're too close to the drain entrance. They could get you with chemical sprays.'

Dully, Limpy realised the slug was right.

'Follow me,' said the slug.

They followed it.

After they'd all travelled along the

drain for a while, and turned off into another drain, Goliath cleared his throat.

'Is it true,' he asked the slug, 'that you blokes sleep in your own snot?'

Normally Limpy would have told Goliath off and apologised to the slug, but right now he just didn't care.

The slug sighed.

'Do you mind?' it said to Goliath. 'I'm feeling a bit emotionally fragile myself at the moment. You cane toads aren't the only ones having a bad week.'

'Sorry,' said Goliath.

Limpy frowned at the slug.

'What do you mean,' he said, 'we're not the only ones?'

'You'll see,' said the slug.

While the three of them trudged through the maze of drains, Limpy peered into the gloom and wondered what the slug had meant by 'you'll see'.

He didn't really care because nothing mattered now that Charm and the others were doomed, but at least being curious kept his mind off the pain of thinking about them.

Sort of.

Except he couldn't see anything but drains.

Then they turned a corner and Limpy realised they were approaching what looked like a wider section of drain. An eerie light flickered from above.

'Where are we?' Limpy asked the slug.

'This section of drain runs under a

pub,' replied the slug. 'That's a place where humans drink beer and forget their troubles and where they live.'

Limpy looked up.

His warts prickled.

Through a grating he could see shapes in a room above them. Human shapes, drinking, silhouetted against the flickering screen of a telly.

'Don't worry,' said the slug. 'They can't see us.'

Limpy hoped the slug was right.

'The tissues are over here,' said a gloomy voice.

Limpy looked around.

It wasn't a human voice.

Suddenly Limpy realised that all around him were animals and insects sitting slumped against the walls of the drain. They all looked as sad and depressed as he felt. Several of them were swigging from bottles with the dull-eyed expressions of folk who weren't really that thirsty.

'Go on,' said the voice. 'Don't be embarrassed.'

A kangaroo was dabbing its eyes with a tissue and holding a couple more out to Limpy and Goliath.

'No thanks,' said Goliath.

'It's OK to be upset,' said the kangaroo. 'I would be if I'd just discovered I was an unloved species.'

'We're not upset,' said Goliath menacingly to the kangaroo. 'And we're not unloved. I love my cousin Limpy and he loves me.'

Limpy nodded. But only for a moment because he was feeling so upset.

The kangaroo was right.

How could I have been so stupid, thought Limpy miserably. How could I have imagined I could have a real friendship with a human? How could I think humans would want to make a fluffy toy out of me?

'Sorry,' the kangaroo was saying. 'Didn't mean to rub it in. If it makes you feel any better, imagine what it's like for me. Humans love me. I'm on the Australian coat of arms. And every travel show ever made about this country. Plus most of the cooking shows. Imagine how I felt when the Games Mascot Committee gave me the thumbs down.’

The kangaroo blew its nose loudly on a tissue.

A koala put its arm round the kangaroo. ‘I know how you feel, mate,’ it said, and took a swig from a bottle.

‘At least they didn’t try and swat you,’ said a blowfly indignantly.

‘Or rush out of the room screaming,’ said a diamond-bellied black snake sadly.

‘Or scratch you off the list,’ said a flea bitterly.

‘I wouldn’t be a mascot now if they came on their hands and knees and begged,’ said a funnel-web spider. ‘Not after all the unkind things they said about me in that committee room.’

‘At least they said them to your face,’ said a crocodile. ‘All I got was a letter.’

‘I wouldn’t be a mascot now if they offered me a million dollars,’ said a wombat.

‘I wouldn’t be one,’ said a blue-tongued lizard, ‘if they offered me a million carports with cracks in the foundations big enough to raise a family in.’

'I wouldn't be one if they offered me a million sticks of sugar cane,' said a cane beetle.

'Or a million sticks,' said Goliath, snatching a tissue and blowing his nose.

Limpy listened to the hurt, indignant voices of the animals and insects around him, and suddenly he felt his warts prickling with anger.

'What I reckon,' he said, 'is that we've all been treated shabbily by our country.'

The other animals and insects fell silent.

They turned to look at Limpy.

'These Games,' continued Limpy, his voice ringing off the wet walls, 'are meant to be about a universal spirit of friendship. That's what they're always saying on telly. Well, the humans haven't shown us much friendship. I reckon we're better off not being a part of such an unfriendly Games. When we look back at all this, I reckon we won't have to feel sad for one minute about not being mascots.'

The animals and insects looked at him, eyes shining.

Then they all burst into mournful cries.

'Yes, we will,' wailed a fruit bat. 'We'll feel sad and worthless for the rest of our lives.'

Limpy turned away, close to wailing himself. He wished he could have been more help.

Oh well, he thought miserably, at least this lot are only feeling flat. At least they won't actually be flat. Not like poor Mum and Dad and Charm and the others at home.

Then Limpy felt a tugging at his elbow. He looked down. It was the cane beetle.

'Don't feel so bad,' said the beetle. 'At least your other country hasn't let you down.'

Limpy looked at the beetle, puzzled. 'What other country?' he said. 'I was born in Australia.'

'Cane toads are from South America,' said the beetle. 'Your ancestors were imported. They were shipped to Australia to eat us cane beetles.'

Limpy tried to digest this.

'That's dopey,' he said. 'You lot live too far off the ground for us to eat you. It's a known fact.'

'Exactly,' said the beetle. 'But the sugar industry blokes who brought you over didn't think of that.'

Limpy's head was spinning.

Imported?

'You're sure you're not confusing us with avocados?' he said.

'Ask that bloke,' said the beetle, pointing at the TV screen in the bar above them. Limpy looked up. On the screen a man was being interviewed.

'He's one of the major sponsors of the Games,' said the beetle. 'One of his companies grows sugar. He'll tell you.'

Limpy's mind was racing.

Thoughts he'd never had before were crashing around inside him.

How dare they?

How dare humans be so cruel to us when we didn't even ask to be here in the first place?

When they brought us here.

It's an injustice.

It's a scandal.

It's not on.

Limpy looked up at the telly screen again.

The Major Sponsor was having a laugh with the interviewer. He looked like a man who was used to getting his own way.

Good, thought Limpy, his warts glowing with anger. Because I need somebody to help me stop this injustice, and I choose you.

'Hang on,' whispered Limpy. 'Corner coming.'

'I don't like it,' said Goliath. 'I want to get off.'

Limpy sighed.

'You didn't have to come,' he whispered. 'I could have done it on my own.'

'I wouldn't have come,' said Goliath sulkily. 'Not if you'd told me I'd have to get this close to a fruit salad. You know I hate fruit.'

'Hide behind the cream trifle then,' whispered Limpy. 'Or the chocolate mousse.'

'I don't like cream or chocolate either,' said Goliath. 'Why can't I hide behind a worm stew?'

'Because,' whispered Limpy, warts prickling with exasperation, 'we're on a dessert trolley. Humans don't eat worm stew for dessert. Not once on telly have I seen a human eat a worm stew for dessert.'

Goliath looked amazed.

'What?' he squeaked. 'Not even with slug topping?'

Limpy slapped his hand over Goliath's mouth. 'Quiet,' he whispered.

The waiter was coming back to the trolley.

Limpy and Goliath clung to the shuddering fruit salad bowl as the trolley was wheeled over the thick restaurant carpet to the next table.

'How long till we get there?' whined Goliath for what Limpy calculated must be the hundred billionth time.

Limpy sighed.

'Not long,' he said.

He peered out from behind the fruit salad bowl.

Three tables to go.

Three tables to the Major Sponsor's table.

'If these humans see us, we're history,' moaned Goliath. 'They might be dressed posh, but they'll still try to beat us to death with their ice-cream spoons.'

'They won't see us,' whispered Limpy. 'Not if you keep quiet and keep your head down.'

Limpy hoped he was right.

Luckily most of the people in the restaurant were staring at a large screen on the stage, where the bloke with the clipboard was showing images of athletes doing athletic things.

Limpy couldn't understand a word the bloke was saying.

He didn't need to. He had a pretty good idea what was going on. The cane beetle had explained it all. How this was a special dinner for all the Games sponsors. So they could find out what world records the Games organisers were hoping would be broken in the various events.

'Why do they want to know that?' Limpy had asked.

'Advertising,' the cane beetle had explained.

Limpy still hadn't understood.

'Here's how it works,' the cane beetle had continued. 'Imagine a TV ad. An athlete in bed with a heavy cold. Cut to the athlete breaking a world record, say for eating sugar cane. Cut to the athlete with a gold medal explaining how XYZ cold and flu tablets clear blocked sinuses in record time. Get it?'

Limpy had got it. And now, as the dessert trolley clattered over to the next table, he had another thought.

Perhaps that's why most humans were so bad-tempered and angry.

Blocked sinuses.

Limpy peered out from behind the fruit salad bowl.

Two tables to go.

Two tables to the Major Sponsor's table.

Limpy felt his warts tighten with nerves. And also tingle with pride. The cane beetle had suggested sneaking in to the sponsor's dinner, but the dessert trolley had been Limpy's idea.

'This dessert trolley idea,' muttered Goliath, 'is dopey.'

Limpy ignored him.

He ran through in his mind what he had to do when they finally got to the

Major Sponsor's table.

First, tell the Major Sponsor about the injustice cane toads were suffering, with special mention of their brains being squeezed out through their ears.

Then, explain how the sugar industry was partly responsible.

Finally, persuade the Major Sponsor to make amends by running heaps of TV ads telling humans that cane toads are really very nice once you get to know them.

Limpy knew it wasn't going to be easy, specially as he didn't speak the Major Sponsor's language.

Everything would depend on how much he could get across to the Major Sponsor by drawing diagrams on the tablecloth in chocolate mousse and strawberry sauce.

Limpy tried to look on the bright side.

Perhaps, he thought hopefully as the trolley clattered to the next table, the girl athlete with the big stick might appear with me in the ads.

At that moment the girl athlete walked onto the stage.

For half a second Limpy thought he was dreaming, that the stress was making him see things.

Then he realised other athletes were walking onto the stage as well. The bloke with the clipboard was introducing them as the athletes who'd been in the presentation. The people at the tables were applauding loudly.

Limpy would have joined in but for one thing.

A woman at a nearby table who'd been asleep had just been woken up by the applause. Limpy saw that she wasn't facing the stage, she was facing the dessert trolley.

Now she was staring.

Now her eyes were bulging and her mouth was opening wide.

Now she was screaming.

Limpy hoped desperately she'd just had a bad dream. He hoped desperately she wasn't screaming at him and Goliath. He hoped desperately she just hated rhubarb pavlova.

Except she wasn't pointing at the rhubarb pavlova, she was pointing at him and Goliath.

Other people were looking.

And yelling.

Almost certainly not at the rhubarb.

Limpy felt the trolley jolt and move off at speed. The waiter had grabbed it and was charging out of the restaurant with it.

As they sped past the Major Sponsor's table, Limpy saw the Major Sponsor frowning at the disappearing trolley. He didn't look like a man who'd want to make amends. Not when he wasn't getting any dessert.

Limpy peered towards the stage, hoping to catch the girl athlete's eye. She was peering quizzically towards the trolley, but Limpy could tell she couldn't really see what was going on.

Then a massive jolt nearly flung Limpy into the raspberry pudding as the trolley crashed through some swing doors.

'Jump!' Limpy yelled at Goliath.

'I can't,' said Goliath. His voice sounded muffled. Limpy saw this was because his head was in the cream trifle.

Then Limpy saw something that churned his stomach even more.

A security guard was running towards them down the corridor with a big snarling black dog on a lead.

The security guard stopped, crouched down, and suddenly the dog wasn't on the lead any more.

With a wet snarl it leapt onto the trolley.

Limpy pressed himself into the cold glass of the fruit salad bowl and tried desperately to look like a piece of rockmelon.

If only he could reach Goliath and push him down into the trifle before the dog saw him.

Too late.

The dog snatched Goliath in its jaws, jumped off the trolley and ran down the corridor.

'Goliath,' screamed Limpy.

The corridor was full of waiters yelling and bumping into each other. The dog darted through them and disappeared.

'Goliath,' sobbed Limpy.

It was no good.

Goliath wouldn't stand a chance in those huge jaws between those massive yellow teeth.

Then Limpy heard something.

A dog barking.

Outside.

The brute must have taken Goliath outside to crunch him up.

Limpy looked wildly around and saw a window in the wall above his head. It was open just a crack. He flung himself at the wall and, helped by the sticky fruit-salad syrup on his hands and feet, dragged himself up it.

He squeezed through the window and launched himself into the darkness.

When he hit the ground, he was dazed for what felt like ages.

A few thoughts stuck in his spinning brain.

Find the dog. Get Goliath out of its mouth. Let the dog chew on my leg if necessary. The crook one preferably.

Then Limpy heard groans.

He opened his eyes, hoping desperately that Goliath was still alive.

But it wasn't Goliath he saw lying on

the grass moaning and dribbling, it was the dog.

'Dopey mongrel,' said a familiar voice.

Limpy spun round.

Goliath was leaning unsteadily against the wall, panting, covered with teeth-marks and trifle.

'Silly bugger bit me in the glands,' he said. 'Squirted himself in the gob.'

Limpy stared, dazed and weak with relief. Then he grabbed Goliath and dragged him towards the bushes. The security guard couldn't be far away.

'Not bad for a bloke with a bad back, eh?' said Goliath. 'That dozy heap'll have a bellyache for a week.'

Limpy didn't say anything. He was putting all his energy into dragging Goliath towards the stormwater drain at the edge of the restaurant garden.

But he knew Goliath was right.

It was amazing.

That dog was bigger than a whole swamp-full of cane toads put together. And Goliath had beaten it.

'It'd take something bigger than a dog to stop me,' Goliath was saying. 'A croc, or maybe a sheep.'

Limpy still didn't say anything.

As they scrambled into the drain, his head was buzzing with an idea.

An idea that could solve all their problems.

An idea that was even bigger than a sheep.

'Me?' said the flea.

Limpy nodded, grinning.

'Me compete in the Games?' said the flea. 'Are you mental?'

The other animals and insects stared at Limpy and shook their heads and feelers. Limpy could see they thought he was.

'It's tragic,' muttered the crocodile sadly. 'The stress of being the ugliest species on the planet has got too much for him and his brain's exploded.'

'Hey,' said Goliath to the crocodile, 'don't insult my cousin, OK? He might be a bit weird-looking but he's not mental.'

'Everybody calm down,' said Limpy, 'and let me explain my idea. No, even better, I'll demonstrate it.' He pointed to the flea. 'Goliath, eat Gavin.'

Goliath looked at the flea, confused.

The flea, alarmed, jumped up onto the ceiling of the drain.

Goliath turned to Limpy. 'You told me I wasn't allowed to eat any of our friends in the drain,' he said.

'That's right,' said Limpy, 'and I'm glad you remembered.' He looked up at the flea. 'Gavin, sorry to startle you but I just wanted us all to see you do your biggest jump.'

'Yeah, well there'd better be a good reason,' said the flea, glaring down at Limpy. 'This stress is not helping my ulcer.'

Goliath was glaring at Limpy too. 'You've got me all hungry now,' he complained.

Limpy took a deep breath.

It wasn't easy getting simple but brilliant ideas across. No wonder cane toads didn't go in much for philosophy, quantum physics or interior decoration.

'OK,' said Limpy. 'Does anyone here know measurements?'

Most of the animals and insects looked at each other and scratched their heads and thoraxes.

'I do,' said a wood worm. 'I once spent a couple of weeks eating a carpenter's ruler.'

'Great,' said Limpy. 'How high would you say Gavin jumped just now?'

The wood worm squinted up at the ceiling. 'About one and a half metres,' she said.

'Thank you,' said Limpy. 'And how tall would you say Gavin is.'

'I know that,' said Gavin. 'I'm good with numbers too. I once spent three days in a maths teacher's armpit. My height is a shade under half a millimetre. My brother Lofty though, you should see him. He's a good tenth of a millimetre taller than me easy.'

'Right,' said Limpy. He took another deep breath. This was the crucial bit. He wished now he'd paid more attention in Ancient Eric's class on How Many Insects Have I Just Eaten?

'If Gavin's half a millimetre tall,' said Limpy, 'and the ceiling's a metre and a half up, that means Gavin just jumped . . . um . . . many, many times higher than his own height.'

'Three thousand times higher,' said Gavin proudly.

'Exactly,' said Limpy. 'Now, that bloke who's the world champion high-jumper at the Games. Anyone know how many times his body height he can jump?'

The animals and insects looked at each other again, frowning.

'Three thousand and one?' said Goliath.

Limpy shook his head.

'About one,' said the wood worm. 'The average human athlete is about two metres tall, and the world record for the human high jump isn't much more than that.'

'Exactly,' said Limpy.

He paused to let this sink in.

The animals and insects gazed up admiringly at Gavin the flea.

'Wow,' said the crocodile to Gavin. 'You're three thousand times better than the human world champion high-jumper. You should compete in the Games.'

'We all should,' said Limpy quietly.

The animals and insects stared at

Limpy, stunned.

'If the world champion weight-lifter at the Games,' said Limpy, 'tried to lift as many times his own body weight as the average ant can lift, he'd be crushed.'

'Jeepers,' said an ant. 'No wonder the humans wouldn't let me be a mascot, they were embarrassed.'

'Crocodiles are better swimmers than humans,' continued Limpy. 'Lizards are better at marathons. Spiders are better sprinters. Kingfishers are better divers. Snakes are better climbers. Kangaroos are better at the hop, step and jump. I've seen head lice do better gymnastics than the best human gymnasts. There's hardly an event at the Games that an animal or insect isn't better at than the human world record-holder.'

The drain echoed with cheers and yells of delight.

'Hang on,' shouted the kangaroo, suddenly frowning. 'It's not that simple. The humans'll never let us compete in their Games.'

Slowly the drain fell silent.

Limpy took a deep breath. His heart was going faster than the pistons in an accelerating truck. This was the best idea he'd ever had.

'That's why,' said Limpy, 'we're going to have our own Games. The Non-Human Games. When the telly networks get a squiz at our world records, they'll be broadcasting our Games quicker than you can say Major Sponsor.'

The animals and insects stared at him, stunned again.

'That's brilliant,' squeaked Gavin the flea. 'When human sports fans see what great athletes we are, we'll be heroes.'

'Or at least,' said Limpy quietly, 'they might stop killing us.'

The drain erupted with cheers again, even louder than before.

Limpy looked around at the delighted animals and insects. He thought of Mum and Dad and Charm and how they'd soon be safe.

His warts tingled with happiness.

Then Limpy realised Goliath was staring at him, eyes shining.

'My own cousin,' said Goliath breathlessly. 'A genius. Wait till they find out at home.'

Limpy couldn't stop himself giving a happy smile.

'So,' continued Goliath. 'What event will us cane toads be setting world records in?'

Limpy felt his smile fading.

It was a good question.

A worrying question.

Kangaroos were better hoppers.

Fleas were better jumpers.

Goliath was strong, but not as strong as an ant.

Eating mud worms and letting them crawl out your bottom wasn't an official event.

Limpy felt the happy tingle slowly disappearing from his warts.

'Well?' asked Goliath, eyes clouding with concern. 'What's our special event?'

'There'll be one,' said Limpy, trying not to look too anxious. 'There's got to be. We just have to find out what it is.'

'It's not water polo,' said Goliath, staggering out of the lake and coughing up pond weed. 'Water polo sucks. Every time I catch the round thing, I sink.'

'We must be doing something wrong,' said Limpy, rubbing the painful lump on his head. 'Maybe at the Games they play it with a ball instead of a rock.'

'I'm fed up,' said Goliath, flopping down in the grass at the edge of the lake. 'I want to go home.'

Limpy sighed.

'We've got to come up with more events to try,' he said. 'We've only tried eleven. Ten not counting wrestling, which wasn't really an event because you were doing it with yourself. Keep thinking.'

Limpy felt awful saying it. Thinking was really hard and painful for Goliath. He could tell by the way Goliath's warts went pale while he did it.

Goliath's warts were pale now and he was frowning and staring into the distance.

'Table tennis,' he was mumbling. 'Rowing. Cricket. Knitting . . .'

Then suddenly his eyes opened wide.

'I've got it,' he said.

Limpy saw that Goliath was staring at a human riding a bike on the other side of the park.

'Good thought,' said Limpy sadly. 'They said on telly that cycling's a really important event. But your feet wouldn't even reach the pedals.'

'I'm not talking about cycling,' said Goliath. 'I'm talking about jamming a stick through the front spokes of that bike. That human'd be on the ground in a heap before you could say, "I'm gunna bash you up you murdering mongrel".'

Limpy sighed again.

'We're trying to make humans like us, remember?' he said. 'I just don't think bashing them up is going to help. Now come on, think of some Games events we haven't tried.'

Goliath scowled. 'This whole idea sucks. We've been in this dumb park all morning. I've got pulled muscles from trying to do gymnastics on the monkey bars, splinters from when that twig archery bow broke, and bruises on my bum from discovering I can't grass ski. I reckon we should forget being Games champions and bash up some humans.'

'I've got a better idea,' said Limpy. 'Come on.'

'Blow up some humans?' said Goliath hopefully as he hopped after Limpy. 'Mess up some humans' hair?'

*   *   *

Limpy carefully pushed up the small grating, clambered out of the drain and helped Goliath squeeze out after him.

'Careful of these tiles,' he said. 'They're wet and slippery.'

He looked around.

Along one wall was a row of lockers, along the other a row of showers.

'Oh yuk,' said Goliath, shuddering. 'Is this where humans wash?'

Limpy nodded. Even though the showers were empty, it was a pretty scary sight.

'I get it,' said Goliath, suddenly excited. 'We've come to steal their soap and shampoo.'

'No,' said Limpy wearily. 'We haven't come to do that.'

'I don't get it then,' said Goliath. 'Why bother breaking into the athletes' changing rooms if we're not gunna strike a blow for cane toads everywhere and mess up their toilet bags?'

'Because,' said Limpy patiently as he led Goliath across the tiles, 'we're here to find the athletics storeroom.'

'And break all the equipment,' said Goliath hopefully.

Limpy wondered if a cold shower would help cool down Goliath's brain.

There wasn't time.

He could hear the crowd cheering outside in the stadium. As soon as the event was over, the changing rooms would be thronging with athletes and Games officials and security guards and big dogs hungry for revenge.

'We have to be quick,' said Limpy as he led Goliath into the next room. 'We need to find some athletics equipment for an event we can be good at. And we have to do it without anyone seeing us.'

'Too late,' said a voice.

Limpy froze.

Goliath bumped into him, then froze.

'Fancy seeing you blokes again,' said the voice.

Limpy looked around, not daring to breathe.

Then his breath squeaked out in a big sigh of relief.

It was the mosquito from the girl athlete's room, lying on a windowsill, legs crossed, wings folded behind his head, grinning at them.

'Sorry if I startled you,' he said. 'I was just having a bit of a lie-down between morning tea and my pre-lunch snack.' The mosquito patted his bulging belly and burped. 'I love the Games.'

'You're lucky,' grumbled Goliath. 'I'm not allowed to eat most of the food around here.'

'Nice to see you again,' said Limpy to the mosquito. 'You'll have to excuse us, we're a bit busy.'

He turned to lead Goliath towards the next room, and froze again.

There, in front of him, was a pile of round, flat objects stacked one on top of the other.

Limpy felt his body start to tremble.

They looked like . . . no, they couldn't be . . .

'Discuses,' said the mosquito. 'Humans chuck 'em. Very popular event, throwing the discus.'

Limpy stared at him as this sank in.

'They're not . . . dead?' he whispered.

The mosquito shook his head. 'Plastic,' he said. 'Be a good event for you blokes.' He looked at Limpy's crook leg. 'Specially you, cause to chuck 'em you have to go round in circles.'

Normally Limpy would have eaten anyone who made a crack about his crook leg, but the mosquito sounded genuinely helpful.

Before Limpy had a chance to explain that he could never throw anything that looked like an uncle, the crowd in the stadium gave a roar.

'Come and see this,' said the mosquito, beckoning to Limpy and Goliath.

They went over and peered through the window.

Far below, in the centre of the stadium, a tiny figure with its hair in a ponytail was running with a big stick held over its head.

'If she gets this jump,' said the mosquito, 'she's in the final.'

Limpy gasped.

It was the girl.

Limpy gazed down at the tiny figure as she jammed the stick into the ground and went soaring high on the end of it, up, up, over the crossbar.

The crowd roared so loudly the window shook.

'She's done it,' yelled the mosquito, dancing around on the windowsill. 'An Aussie pole-vaulter's in the final. Great little athlete, that one. I've bitten her heaps.'

Limpy couldn't take his eyes off the girl as she waved delightedly to the crowd.

That could be me, he thought. If only . . .

His dreams were shattered by the sound of dogs barking and human voices shouting.

Close.

Very close.

'Oops,' said the mosquito. 'I forgot to mention. After your little stunt at the dinner the other night, cane toads are public enemy number one around here. Kill on sight, I think I heard the security chief say. Good luck. Oh, if you see any deodorant, bung it on. At the moment those dogs can smell you miles away.'

The mosquito buzzed out a window up near the ceiling. The only window in the room, Limpy saw, that wasn't sealed.

It was too high to hop up to.

The dogs were getting closer.

'Oh no,' croaked Goliath. 'I've only had experience with one dog. One dog's all I can cope with. I'm hopeless with packs.'

Limpy's brain was racing.

There wasn't even time to get back to the shower room.

'I can't see any deodorant,' Goliath was shouting, rummaging through toilet bags in a frenzy. 'We're going to die.'

Then Limpy saw two sticks leaning against the wall next to the high window. They were long thin sticks, each with a metal hook on the end for opening and closing the window.

Limpy grabbed them and pushed one into Goliath's hands.

Suddenly he knew what to do.

The drain was cold and full of car fumes, and the water had smelly blobs of chemical factory sludge and congealed cooking fat floating in it.

Limpy didn't care.

All he could think of as he splashed along next to Goliath was the wonderful feeling.

The wonderful soaring feeling.

OK, at first it had been a terrified feeling. As Limpy had sprinted across the changing-room floor, stick held above his head, he'd felt himself starting to veer off to one side. He knew that if the veer turned into a circle, he'd crash into the pile of discuses and still be dragging himself out from under them when the guard dogs arrived.

He could hear them getting closer.

They sounded bigger than the one at the restaurant. Fiercer too probably, and specially trained not to swallow anything that came out of a toad's glands.

Limpy begged his crook leg to stay strong.

Although he was still veering, he didn't crash into the discuses.

Instead, he jammed the far end of his stick under a bench, gripped his end and flung himself upwards in the biggest hop of his life.

He felt the stick bend as he went upwards and then, miraculously, straighten out again and carry him soaring, soaring, through the high window.

Even after he let go of the stick, he carried on soaring, arms wide, yelling with fear and excitement and so much joy he didn't know how he could ever feel more joyful. Until he saw Goliath soaring next to him, eyes bulging and tongue plastered across his face, and did.

'Yes!'

Limpy heard his voice echoing down

the drain and realised he was yelling joyfully again now, just remembering it.

He turned excitedly to Goliath.

'Wasn't it brilliant?' he said. 'Wasn't it the most wonderful, brilliant, fantastic thing you've ever done?'

'No,' said Goliath.

It's shock, thought Limpy. He's in shock from the excitement.

'It's all right for you,' said Goliath. 'You landed on nice soft grass, not in a hard rubbish bin full of really sharp sandwich wrappers.'

Limpy watched sympathetically as Goliath pulled a fragment of plastic out of his scalp, studied it glumly, and ate it.

'I hate pole vaulting,' said Goliath. 'It's scary and it hurts.'

'It won't always be like that,' said Limpy. 'When we're doing it in a stadium, there'll be soft mats to land on.'

Goliath didn't reply.

Limpy saw he'd picked up a handful of something green and oozy from the water.

'Is this chemical factory sludge or

congealed cooking fat? asked Goliath. 'I'm starving.'

Poor old Goliath, thought Limpy. He'll cheer up when he sees how delighted the other animals and insects are that we've found our special event.

* * *

The animals and insects didn't seem that delighted.

'Um,' said the kangaroo to Limpy and Goliath, 'I'm afraid there's something we have to tell you, and, well, um . . .'

The kangaroo looked unhappily at the koala, who stared at the drain wall and pretended to be thinking about something else.

Limpy couldn't believe it.

He'd just finished telling all the animals and insects about the pole vaulting, complete with actions and yells and a detailed description of how brave Goliath was after he landed in the rubbish bin, and now, as he looked around at all their faces, not a single one was pleased or excited.

‘It’s like this,’ said the kangaroo, ‘um . . .’

An awful thought hit Limpy.

Someone else must have chosen pole vaulting.

A wombat or a jellyfish or a stick insect.

Limpy opened his mouth to explain how the highly-developed hopping muscles in a cane toad’s legs and the superb gripping qualities of a cane toad’s hands were a perfect combination for pole vaulting, but he didn’t get a chance.

‘We’ve had a meeting,’ said the kangaroo. ‘A meeting with some head-lice we know who work in television. They think the Non-Human Games idea sounds great, really exciting, but there is . . . um . . . a problem.’

Several of the other animals and insects murmured their agreement.

Limpy felt wobbly with relief.

At least no one else wanted to do pole vaulting.

At least he and Goliath could be the ones to break all the pole-vaulting records and become national sporting heroes, and make cane toads popular and loved.

At least it wasn't a big problem.

'The problem is,' said the kangaroo, 'we've decided you two can't be in the Games.'

The other animals and insects all growled their agreement.

Limpy stared at them, bewildered.

Goliath took a menacing step towards the kangaroo.

'Why not?' he said. 'What have you got against me and my cousin.'

'It's not the leg,' said the kangaroo hastily, backing away and glancing guiltily at Limpy. 'It definitely has nothing to do with the crook leg, you must believe that. And we do acknowledge that the whole thing was your idea, and we're very grateful for that.'

'So what is it?' said Limpy, suddenly filled with a mixture of anger and dread. 'Spit it out.'

'The reason we can't have any cane toads in our televised Non-Human Games,' said the kangaroo, 'is that you're too ugly.'

'Ugly,' said Goliath, pacing up and down. 'What do they mean, I'm ugly?'

Now that all the animals and insects had gone, his voice echoed indignantly around the empty drain.

Limpy sighed sadly.

'Lazy I could understand,' continued Goliath, 'or smelly, or maybe even greedy, but ugly? I don't get it.'

Limpy sighed again.

If I had the energy, he thought miserably, I'd probably tell Goliath to calm down.

Because what does it matter now?

Most of the humans in the world think cane toads are ugly and vile and repulsive, so what does it matter if most of the animals and insects do too?

We're history, that's all that matters.

'I reckon they're just jealous,' said

Goliath bitterly. 'Jealous they haven't got warts.'

'Goliath,' said Limpy wearily, 'sit down.'

'I can't,' said Goliath. 'I'm too upset. Right now I'm probably the most upset individual on the planet.'

Limpy was about to say 'actually, you're not,' when another voice said it first.

Limpy stared.

A slug was crawling towards them.

Limpy's first impulse was to eat it. Then he recognised its friendly face. It was the slug who had brought them there in the first place.

'Why aren't you off training with the others?' said Limpy.

'They don't want me in their Games,' said the slug sadly. 'They say I'm too slimy.'

'Bad luck,' said Limpy.

'Yeah,' said Goliath. 'Very upsetting for you. But I'm still the most upset.'

'Actually,' said the slug, 'I think she is.'

He pointed upwards with a feeler.

Limpy looked up. Through the

grating he could see the telly screen flickering in the bar above them. On the screen was the girl. She was talking to an interviewer and struggling to hold back tears.

'She's just been banned from competing in the pole-vaulting final,' said the slug. 'She failed the blood test.'

'What blood test?' said Limpy.

'Athletes get tested to make sure they haven't got any drugs or chemicals in their blood,' said the slug. 'Stuff that'll enhance their performance. They found some sort of weird steroid in hers. She says she doesn't know how it got there. It's a prohibited substance so she's automatically banned.'

'Serves her right for cheating,' said Goliath. 'I reckon cheats should be run over by trucks.'

Limpy turned away from the screen. Humans, he thought sadly. Even the good ones turn out to be dud.

'Actually,' said the slug, 'she might not have been cheating. Certain poisons and venoms contain steroids. Perhaps she was bitten by a snake or something.'

Limpy stared at the slug.

His mind was racing.

It raced all the way back to the park where the girl had taken him after rescuing him from the teenagers in the loading dock.

He'd accidentally scratched her hand.

Could some of his poison have got into her blood?

It was possible.

Limpy looked back up at the screen. The bloke with the clipboard was being interviewed now, red-faced and angry.

Then the girl again, looking even sadder than before.

Watching her, Limpy felt his own throat tighten.

It would be difficult, paying her back for saving him.

And scary.

And very dangerous.

I don't care, he thought wearily.

So far this month I've failed to save my species, I haven't even been able to protect my own mum and dad and sister, and I'll probably be flattened by a truck myself sooner or later.

I want to do one good thing before I die.

Limpy could hear the girl sobbing on her bed as he and Goliath clambered in through the bathroom window and dropped into the bath.

'This is crazy,' muttered Goliath. 'This is gunna end with us having wet cheeks too, except it'll be dog slobber.'

Limpy reached up and put his hands on Goliath's shoulders.

He took a deep breath so his voice wouldn't wobble. This was the most important thing he'd ever said to Goliath, and big cousins sometimes didn't take you seriously if your voice was wobbling.

'Goliath,' said Limpy, 'I want you to stay here.'

Goliath's mouth flopped open.

'I mean it,' said Limpy firmly.

'No way,' said Goliath. 'I'm not

letting you go off to be dog meat on your own.'

Limpy took another deep breath. This was exactly what he'd expected Goliath to say.

He looked hard into Goliath's eyes.

'I need you to stay here,' he said. 'Dad will have put the word around by now that I'm on a mission to stop humans killing cane toads. The folks at home don't know I've failed. They don't know they still have to watch out for cars and trucks. It's really important that one of us gets back to warn them.'

Limpy paused while Goliath digested this.

'I'm sure I'll be OK,' he went on, 'but just in case I'm not, you'll have to go back on your own. Get a cockroach to direct you to the city market, find a truck with mangoes painted on the side and stow away.'

Goliath swallowed, and Limpy saw that his cousin's warts were quivering with emotion.

'They're all depending on you Goliath,' he said.

Goliath didn't say anything, and Limpy realised that Goliath was struggling with a voice wobble of his own.

Limpy squeezed Goliath's shoulders, then turned and hopped out of the bath.

He didn't say goodbye.

No point upsetting them both.

* * *

The girl was lying face down on the bed, sobbing into her pillow.

Limpy hopped up onto the bedspread and nudged her arm with his shoulder.

She rolled over and opened her eyes.

Limpy hopped round in circles a few times so she'd know it was him and not just any cane toad who happened to be passing.

For a long time she just stared at him, blinking through her tears.

Then her face broke into an amazed grin.

'What are you doing here?'

Limpy could tell she'd recognised

him.

Now, he thought, for the tricky bit.

He hopped over and touched her hand with his toenails, careful not to scratch her this time. Then he mimed his own hand hurting, sucking it and blowing on it and waving it around like a truck had just run over it.

He only had to do it for a while before he saw her eyes widen and her mouth fall open and delighted understanding creep across her face.

*   *   *

The Games officials understood immediately.

It took them a while to believe her, though.

Limpy watched as the girl talked animatedly to them and pointed to him and to her hand and mimed a small amount of poison flowing through her blood.

At least, he imagined that's what she was doing. It was pretty hard to see from inside the plastic bag the officials had put him in. The plastic bag had previously had some sort of orange smoked fish in it, and the sides were all smeary and hard to see through.

Limpy rubbed till he had a clear patch.

He watched as the officials kept shaking their heads, right up until the girl grabbed a handful of newspapers and waved them threateningly under their noses.

Then, unhappily, they nodded.

* * *

The lab was very bright.

Limpy squinted, partly from the lights and partly from fear.

He knew what could happen to animals in labs.

Please, he begged silently as a man in a white coat put him on a white bench. Please let this human know how to get poison out of a cane toad without any cutting or lethal injections.

Trembling, Limpy wondered if he should help the man.

Squirt at him, just a bit.

He decided not to.

The man put on rubber gloves and plastic goggles and squeezed one of Limpy's glands. Pus plopped into a glass bowl.

Limpy felt so weak with relief that he didn't even struggle when the man put him into a glass tank and put a lid on it.

Instead, he watched through the side of the tank as the man did things on the bench with glass tubes and bits of equipment Limpy didn't recognise. Not much lab equipment got chucked out of cars in North Queensland.

The girl and the officials watched too.

Finally, the man in the white coat turned to the girl.

'You're clear,' he said.

Limpy didn't understand at first, not until the girl came grinning over to the tank, took the lid off, and gave him a big kiss.

*   *   *

Later, after Limpy had got over his disappointment about the girl putting the lid back on the tank and leaving without him, he decided it was time to escape.

Later still, after he'd climbed up the wall of the tank about a million times and tried to push the lid off about a million times and fallen on his head about a million times, he realised he couldn't.

Then the lab filled up with humans in white coats, all staring up at a telly on the wall.

On the screen, Limpy saw the girl.

She was in the middle of the stadium, soaring over a crossbar that looked even higher than before.

All the humans in the lab started cheering and hugging each other.

Then they left.

Limpy smiled.

He was glad the girl had made them cheer. She must have done well.

Perhaps she'll come back and kiss me again, thought Limpy hopefully. And then take me back to Goliath.

He waited, not hoping too hard in case she didn't.

A long time passed. Even though he didn't want to, Limpy found himself thinking sadly about Charm.

Then he realised with a start that someone was standing behind the tank, watching him.

It wasn't the girl.

Limpy's insides sank as he saw a clipboard and a red face with hard, shiny eyes.

The bloke in the suit reached into the tank and lifted Limpy out and held him up and stared at him with a thin-lipped expression. Limpy felt pretty sure that whatever was going to happen next wouldn't involve a kiss.

Limpy had never been on a winner's podium at a Games before, and he felt a bit overwhelmed.

It was partly the noise.

A stadium full of humans applauding and cheering was the loudest thing Limpy had ever heard, including some pretty big thunderstorms back home.

Another reason was that he was still in shock.

When the bloke with the clipboard had hurried out of the lab with Limpy in a manila envelope, Limpy had been pretty sure they were heading for somewhere unpleasant.

A loading dock perhaps.

Or a highway so the bloke could run Limpy over in his car.

So when the bloke hurried into the stadium and handed Limpy to the girl just before she stepped onto the podium and received her gold medal, Limpy had been pretty surprised.

The main reason he was a bit overwhelmed, though, was what was happening to him now.

The girl was holding Limpy over her head and the humans in the stadium were cheering even louder.

At him.

Stack me, thought Limpy. I think they like me.

*   *   *

Phew, thought Limpy as the girl carried him into the boardroom, it's all go being a national hero.

The girl had barely had time for a shower and Limpy had barely had time for a drink of water, and now the bloke with the clipboard was rushing them into a meeting.

Limpy didn't know what the meeting was about, but he hoped it would go on long enough for him to catch his breath.

The girl sat at the head of a long

table and put Limpy down in front of her.

Limpy looked around.

There were several humans seated at the table and they were all grinning at him.

Limpy swallowed nervously.

He knew he should like it, but it felt weird.

The bloke with the clipboard took a seat at the other end of the table and started talking.

Limpy couldn't understand what he was saying, but he was obviously very enthusiastic about something. It seemed to be Limpy.

Then one of the other humans held up some sheets of drawing paper and Limpy became very enthusiastic as well.

They were sketches of cane toads.

In display bins.

In shops.

Stack me, thought Limpy delightedly.

Fluffy cane toad toys.

It's happened.

We're saved.

Limpy had a wonderful vision of every vehicle in Australia with a fluffy brushed-polyester cane toad hanging from its rear-vision mirror. A cute, lovable fluffy cane toad that would remind the driver to be very careful not to run over any cute, lovable real cane toads.

Not Charm, not Goliath, not any of them.

Limpy felt like doing cartwheels. He felt like kissing everyone round the table.

Instead he looked up gratefully at the girl. She was grinning happily too.

Then her grin faded.

Limpy turned round and saw why.

At the other end of the table, the bloke with the clipboard was holding up a fluffy cane toad toy for the other humans to examine.

Except, Limpy saw as he stared in horror, it wasn't fluffy.

It wasn't even a toy.

It was the dry stuffed skin of a real cane toad.

Limpy felt sick and dizzy.

He struggled with his breathing

while the other humans passed the stuffed corpse among themselves, obviously delighted. The only voice raised in protest, Limpy was dimly aware, was the girl's.

He couldn't see her expression.

He couldn't take his eyes off the bloke with the clipboard, who was standing next to a map of Australia on the wall. He picked up the stuffed corpse and pointed to North Queensland with a smile.

The bloke spoke some words and Limpy, sick with horror and despair, knew exactly what they meant.

'Plenty more where this one came from.'

‘Let me get this straight,’ said Goliath.

He was speaking loudly so Limpy could hear him over the hubbub of journalists and TV crews on the other side of the curtain.

‘We’re gunna go onstage at this international press conference, a press conference being held specially to introduce Australia’s new most-loved species, i.e. us, to the world, and be disgusting.’

‘More than disgusting,’ said Limpy. ‘We’re going to show the world just how vile, revolting and repugnant cane toads really are.’

Goliath frowned. Then understanding crept slowly across his big warty face.

Limpy looked up at the girl and gave her a nod.

Holding Limpy in one hand and

Goliath in the other, the girl stepped through the curtain onto the stage.

Limpy was almost blinded by flashing cameras and glaring TV lights.

The girl put him and Goliath down on a table in front of her.

Limpy noticed that most of the cameras were pointing at him and Goliath rather than her.

Good, he thought.

With an encouraging grin to both of them, the girl opened the tin of mud worms they'd spent all morning collecting. She tipped them out onto the table.

As he picked the first one up and dropped it wriggling and alive into his mouth, Limpy noticed some of the journalists and cameramen screwing up their faces.

By the time he and Goliath had half a dozen worms each wriggling down their throats, Limpy was pleased to see some of the cameras being turned away and some of the journalists looking a bit ill.

He could tell they were going right off the idea that cane toads were lovable.

The international market for stuffed cane toads, thought Limpy with grim satisfaction, will be history in about two minutes.

He turned round so the journalists all had a good view of his bottom.

Limpy sat in the middle of the highway and let the warm North Queensland night air caress his skin and soothe the sore armpits he'd got from two days on the back of a mango truck.

It was good to be home.

Then he heard a distant rumble.

This is it, he thought, warts suddenly prickling with tension.

A vehicle was approaching at speed.

Limpy looked anxiously up at Goliath, who was sitting next to him on the bitumen. Goliath met his eyes for a moment.

'Here goes,' muttered Goliath.

Limpy looked even more anxiously down at Charm, who was sitting on the other side of him.

'I love you, Limpy,' said Charm. 'I'm saying it now in case we don't get a chance afterwards.'

Limpy stroked her cheek and felt his insides glow with love for her. And his crook leg ached with anxiety.

He held his breath.

The vehicle, a huge semi, was almost at the crossing.

Limpy gripped his stick and faced the oncoming headlights, grim and determined.

Out of the corner of his eye he saw Goliath raise his stick.

'Come and get us, you mongrels,' yelled Goliath.

Limpy, trembling, wanted to grab Charm and hop for the grass verge, but he didn't.

He saw Charm raise her stick.

The truck thundered over the crossing.

Limpy stayed glued to the spot as Goliath raised himself up to his full height and waved his stick at the truck bearing down on them and yelled a torrent of swear words at it.

Limpy's heart was pounding so hard his warts were aching.

'Now,' he yelled.

He watched as Charm planted one end of her stick on the bitumen, just like they'd practised, gripped the other end, flung herself upwards and pole vaulted through the air.

Limpy did the same. Just before he landed on the grass at the edge of the highway, he looked back desperately to make sure Goliath had too. But all he could see was a cloud of dust as the truck roared past.

'Charm,' yelled Limpy. 'Goliath.'

He was still yelling as the truck disappeared into the distance and the dust settled.

Charm stuck her head out of a clump of grass, grinning.

Goliath dropped down from the paperbark tree he'd landed in.

'It works,' he yelled. 'Good on you, Limpy.'

Limpy grinned too, dizzy with relief.

The other cane toads broke into excited applause and crowded round the three of them.

Limpy glowed happily as Dad gave him a proud slap on the back.

Mum hugged him, face shining with

love.

Even Ancient Eric shook his hand.

'It's just as I predicted, young Limpy,' he said. 'You've brought peace and security to cane toads for countless generations to come.'

He glanced nervously down at his stomach.

Limpy smiled.

Then Charm came over and put her arms round him. 'I've worked out why humans don't like us,' she said.

'Why?' said Limpy, gazing down at her dear warty face, and feeling his insides tingle with so much love he thought his eyes were going to do that wet thing humans' eyes did.

'Because,' she said, 'they're jealous they haven't got a big brother like you.'

While Limpy handed sticks out to everyone who wanted to have a go for themselves, he heard Goliath talking to some little cane toads.

'Have I ever met a human?' he was saying. 'Hey, I've had a bath with one.'

Limpy smiled as the little cane toads gasped.

Then he felt a tug at his leg.

A little cane toad was looking up at him.

'Uncle Limpy,' said the little cane toad. 'Why do humans hate us?'

Limpy stared, taken aback. Then he took a deep breath and drew himself up to his full height, like an uncle should. He hoped it didn't matter that he was leaning slightly to one side.

'Well,' Limpy was about to say, 'it's like this. Humans have hated cane toads since the dawn of time and they probably always will. We just have to accept it, like we have to accept that flying insects are attracted to highway lights and crawling insects are attracted to wombat poo. It's just the way things are. Don't worry your little head about it.'

But he didn't say that.

Instead he put his arm round the little cane toad's shoulders. 'That's a good question,' he said. 'Humans claim they hate us cause we're ugly, but I don't reckon that's the whole story. They're a pretty complicated species, humans, and a lot more research needs to be done on them.'

The little cane toad's eyes widened. 'And you think I could be the one to do it? You think one day I could be a brave adventurer like you, risking my life to bring peace and whadyacallit to cane toads for countless thingummies to come and stuff?'

Limpy hopped back in alarm.

The little cane toad wasn't just little, it was very little.

'I wasn't necessarily saying that,' said

Limpy anxiously.

But the little cane toad wasn't listening. It was frowning and looking doubtful. 'Hot water makes my warts itch,' it said. 'I could never have a bath with a human.'

Limpy wondered whether he should mention cold taps. Then the little cane toad's eyes widened again. 'I know,' it shouted happily. 'I'll do a wee in the water to cool it down.'

Limpy watched the little cane toad hop away, its face shining with excitement.

He realised he didn't feel anxious any more.

Stack me, thought Limpy with a chuckle to himself. It's not just half-squashed cane toads that go round in circles.

Life does too.